D0120434

BOARDROOM
BABY SURPRISE

BOARDROOM BABY SURPRISE

BY
JACKIE BRAUN

First published in Great Britain 2009
Large Print edition 2009
Harlequin Mills & Boon Limited,
Eton House, 18-24 Paradise Road,
Richmond, Surrey TW9 1SR

© Jackie Braun Fridline 2009

ISBN: 978 0 263 20648 7

Set in Times Roman 17½ on 22 pt.
16-1209-38966

Harlequin Mills & Boon policy is to use papers that are
natural, renewable and recyclable products and made
from wood grown in sustainable forests. The logging and
manufacturing process conform to the legal environmental
regulations of the country of origin.

Printed and bound in Great Britain
by CPI Antony Rowe, Chippenham, Wiltshire

For my boys, Daniel and Will

CHAPTER ONE

SEATED in the tastefully decorated reception area at Windy City Industries, Morgan Stevens gripped the upholstered arm of the chair and panted as discreetly as she could.

Breathe, she coached herself. In...out... and again.

The jagged edge of the contraction was just beginning to wear off when the secretary returned through one of a trio of doors on the opposite wall.

The name on the woman's desk plate was Britney. It suited her to a T. She was young, attractive, model-slender and crisply fashionable in a fitted black suit, bold-print silk blouse and a pair of killer heels. In comparison, Morgan felt decidedly dowdy in her pastel-colored maternity tent and the comfortable flat sandals that were the only shoes that would accommodate her swollen feet.

"I'm sorry, but Mr. Caliborn is busy and can't see you," Britney said, working up a smile that looked about as sincere as a shark's. "Might I suggest you make an appointment before coming by next time?"

Why? So he could be conveniently gone when she got there? No way. Morgan had been trying to reach Bryan Caliborn for months. She laid a hand on her protruding midsection. Nearly nine of them. The only correspondence she'd had in return, if it could be called such, was a letter from his legal counsel advising her that Mr. Caliborn disputed her allegation of paternity. In fact, he disputed knowing her.

He considered her claims nothing less than extortion, and he would sue for damages if she continued to make them.

More than hurt and insulted by his threat, Morgan was outraged. If he didn't want to play a role in their child's life, fine. He should just say so. But to say they'd never met, well, that was beyond defense, legal or otherwise. She never would have taken Bryan Caliborn for such a ruthless, heartless man. Nor had he seemed slow, but he had to be if he wasn't aware that all it would take was a bit of DNA to confirm Morgan was telling the truth. She'd hoped, apparently in vain, to avoid that sort of ugliness.

Rising awkwardly to her feet, she returned the young woman's smile with one that was equally insincere. "Fine. Please pencil me in for his earliest availability."

"Let me just check his calendar and see when that might be," Britney said.

Morgan saw no sense in arguing with the secretary. She would deal with the elusive businessman herself. And she would do so now. While Britney walked behind her desk, Morgan headed to the door through which the woman had appeared a moment earlier. She assumed it was Bryan's office. Opening it, however, she found it was a conference room, a conference room that was filled with suit-clad professionals seated around an oblong cherry table. File folders were open in front of them, not that they were looking at the pie charts and bar graphs. They were gaping at Morgan. But it was the man at the far end of the room who held her attention.

Handsome? No. A better word would be *arresting*. He had dark, almost black hair and eyes of the same fathomless hue. His face was angular with sharp cheekbones and slashing brows that, at the moment, were pulled down in a frown. The nose above his sculpted, flesh-toned lips was thin and just crooked enough to give it character.

Morgan swallowed. Even seated, it was obvious he was tall and powerfully built. Never in her life had she been attracted to the dark and brooding sort, but something about this man was definitely appealing. She told herself it was only because he seemed oddly familiar.

That thought shattered when he spoke. She'd never heard a voice like that before. He didn't break the silence so much as pulverize it. His words boomed through the room like a thunderclap when he demanded, "What is the meaning of this?"

"Sorry," she began, backing up a step only to bump into the secretary, who took Morgan's arm. The gesture seemed more like an effort to detain rather than to steady her, which irritated Morgan enough to prompt her to say, "I need to speak with Bryan Caliborn, and I need to speak to him right now. I thought he might be in here."

"He is." All eyes turned to the big man at the end of the table, who was now rising to his feet. He was every bit of six-four, maybe six-five, and every inch of him radiated power and authority. Again she had the odd feeling that she knew him, but it came as an utter shock when he said, "I'm Bryan Caliborn."

"No." Morgan shook her head, sure that she had heard him wrong. "You're n—"

She didn't finish the sentence. Her water broke, releasing in a gush to form an unbecoming puddle on the polished parquet floor. The secretary let go of Morgan's arm and jumped back, anxious to protect her Marc Jacobs pumps from harm. The people seated around the table gasped in unison, pulling back in their seats, as if Morgan's condition were contagious. Only the man who claimed to be Bryan moved. Swearing richly half under his breath, he stalked around the table toward her.

"Sorry," Morgan whispered, though she felt more mortified than apologetic.

She would have left then, turned and run away—or waddled as the case may be—but as her luck would have it, another contraction began to build. She angled away from him, hoping to make it to the reception area's couch to wait out the worst of it. She made it only one step before grabbing the door frame and sagging against it. Using the other hand to support her abdomen, she fought the urge to whimper. Nothing was going as planned. Nothing *had* gone as planned in a long, long time.

"Britney, call an ambulance," the big man barked. To Morgan he said, "I take it you're in labor."

Labor? She was being wrenched apart from the inside out. None of the books she'd read, none of the classes she'd taken had prepared her for this kind of pain. But she nodded, worried that any attempt at speech would release not only a whimper but a wailing shriek. God, she hurt.

She needed to sit down. She needed some of the drugs she'd learned about in her birthing class. She needed her mother. Only one of those things was an option now, but before Morgan could wilt to the floor, she was scooped up in a pair of powerful arms and carried into the office that was one door down from the conference room.

He settled her on the leather couch and returned a moment later with what looked to be a balled-up trench coat and a glass of water. He positioned the trench behind her head on the arm rest and then thrust the glass at her.

Morgan wasn't interested in water. For that matter, she doubted she could keep it down. But she dutifully took it and pretended to sip from the glass. His rigid demeanor told her he wasn't the sort of man who stood for being defied. And while she generally wouldn't stand for being bullied, she was in no shape to put him in his place.

"The ambulance will be here any moment," the secretary said, peeking around the semi-closed door.

"An ambulance really isn't necessary," Morgan began. Not to mention that it would be expensive for someone who had just lost her health insurance along with her teaching job when the school year had ended a week earlier. The economy being what it was, the district didn't have the funds for extras like music.

The worst of the contraction had passed, so she swung her legs over the edge of the couch and planted her feet on the floor. She would go now, exiting as gracefully as her condition allowed. Her car was in the parking ramp adjacent to the building and she could be at Chicago's Northwestern Memorial Hospital in less than twenty minutes, assuming the traffic lights and her finicky compact car cooperated.

What stopped her wasn't the big man, even though he took a lurching step in her direction, but the framed picture on the wall just to the right of the door. In it two men stood arm in arm, one dark and brooding, the other fairer and far less serious. Morgan blinked. She knew those smiling eyes, that windblown brown hair and carefree expression. By turns sweet and silly, this was the man with whom she'd spent seven lovely and, for her, uncharacteristically reckless days in Aruba.

Bryan.

She must have said the name aloud because when she glanced over, the man's gaze also was on the photograph, his mouth compressed into a line so tight that it was hard to tell where his top lip ended and the bottom one began.

"You do know him," she accused, pointing to the photograph. "You do know Bryan Caliborn."

"*I* am Bryan Caliborn," he proclaimed a second time. "That's Dillon, my younger brother."

Dillon…

Brother…

The words registered slowly, poking through a haze of disbelief. Though a part of her wanted to dispute them, the proof—all six-feet-something of it—was literally standing before her, his arms crossed, his expression ominous and intractable.

Bryan…rather, Dillon—the man who'd

fathered Morgan's baby, hadn't given her his real name. This wasn't exactly the kind of revelation a woman needed to hear with motherhood a few centimeters and a couple of hard pushes away. It made Morgan wonder what else he had lied about. What other truths he had obscured with his beguiling kisses and those impeccable manners she'd found every bit as seductive as his smile.

In her best schoolteacher's voice, she demanded, "I want to see him." For good measure, she added, "And don't you dare tell me I need to make an appointment. As you can see, I'm not in any condition to wait an hour let alone a week or two."

"It's not possible," the real Bryan had the audacity to say. She opened her mouth, intending to let loose with a blistering retort. Before she could, though, he said, "Dillon's dead."

Anger abandoned her, evaporating like

water on hot asphalt. Bewilderment took its place—bewilderment and a couple dozen other emotions that swirled around in a dizzying mix. Since her legs threatened to give, Morgan backed up to the couch, sinking onto its cushions.

"He's dead?"

Bryan's head jerked down in a nod.

"But how? When?" She asked the questions, needing to know even though the answers really didn't matter. What would they change? Not only was she about to become a single mother, her baby would never know his or her father. She swallowed a fresh wave of nausea. For that matter *she* hadn't known her baby's father.

"Six months ago. A skiing accident in Vail, Colorado." The words came out stilted, made curt by grief. Or was that some other emotion lurking in those onyx eyes?

"I…I didn't know."

"Neither did I." He glanced meaningfully at her stomach. "Where did you and Dillon meet?"

"Aruba. Last August."

She'd gone there alone, using the tickets she'd bought her folks for their thirtieth wedding anniversary. They'd never had a honeymoon. Morgan had wanted to give them one as a surprise. Before she could, though, they'd died in a fluke carbon monoxide accident at their home. Though she wasn't one to make excuses for her behavior, her grief helped explain why someone as level-headed as she usually was had fallen for the faux Bryan's advances in the first place. She'd been lost, lonely. He'd been charming and a distraction from bitter reality.

"And you…spent time with my brother?" One brow arched in disapproval as Bryan once again glanced at her abdomen.

"Yes."

If she'd felt awkward and conspicuous before, she felt doubly so now. She stood, intent on leaving this time, though where exactly she would go beyond the hospital she hadn't a clue. She was between jobs, between homes and in a strange city without family.

A pair of emergency medical technicians arrived before Morgan could get to the door. They carried black bags and were pushing a gurney.

She held up a hand. "Oh, this really isn't necessary. I can get to the hospital on my own steam. My contractions aren't that close together."

Even as she said this another one began. Just how many minutes had passed since the last? She didn't dare chance a glance at her wrist now.

"It is necessary," Bryan objected. "Assuming what you say is true, that child is a Caliborn."

"Assuming—" She gritted her teeth, and not because of the contraction. She would have stalked out then, but one of the technicians, a kind-faced man with salt-and-pepper hair and a bushy mustache, laid a hand on her arm.

"Let's have a look at you first, okay? We wouldn't want you to have that baby while you're stuck in traffic on Michigan Avenue."

He reminded Morgan of her father, which was the only reason she let him lead her back to the couch.

Once she was seated, the EMT knelt in front of her and pulled a blood-pressure cuff from his bag. As it inflated over her upper arm, she glanced at Bryan, who stared back at her stone-faced. She was coming to know that expression. She could only imagine what he was thinking.

Damn Dillon! Damn him for doing this. And damn him for being dead!

Bryan wanted to throttle his little brother, pin him in a chokehold like he used to do when they were kids and pound some sense into him. Only he couldn't. Knowing that reopened a wound that had just barely begun to heal. Why did Dillon have to go and get himself killed?

Bryan still couldn't quite wrap his mind around the fact that Dill was gone, buried in the family plot at Winchester Memorial Gardens alongside their paternal grandparents and a spinster great-aunt. How was it possible for someone that vibrant and full of life to die? Half the time Bryan wanted to believe that his younger brother was simply off on another one of his irresponsible jaunts, charging his good time to Bryan's accounts.

He'd done that often enough after burning through his own trust fund by his late twenties, Vail being the last wild excursion.

Bryan had been furious when his credit card company had called to confirm the charges. Only the best accommodations and restaurants for his little brother. He'd dialed Dill at the luxury hotel where he was staying in a suite that was costing Bryan a few grand a night, and left him a blistering message.

"Grow up, already!" he'd shouted into the receiver. "You're thirty, for God's sake. You have a position at the company if you'd ever deign to work. You need to start earning your own way and stop mooching off me. You do it again and I swear, Dill, I'll call the police."

Of course, he wouldn't have. But he'd been so furious.

Now, sitting in his office looking both terrified and lovely as she answered the EMT's questions and cringed her way through another contraction, was one doozy of an example of his little brother's foolishness. As per usual, it would be up to Bryan to clean up the mess. He'd done that Dill's entire life. Apparently, that applied posthumously, too.

He scrubbed a hand across his eyes. This mess was going to be harder than the others, assuming Morgan wasn't lying about her baby's paternity. That was a possibility given the Caliborn family's net worth. She probably thought she had a big payout coming. Given the state of his brother's finances, she was in for a rude awakening. Unfortunately, determining the truth wasn't as easy as requesting a DNA test. It wasn't because the father in question was deceased. Bryan's DNA could be used to confirm a biological link between the baby and the Caliborns. That was precisely what had him hesitating. He was in no hurry to go through that…again.

He had to say, Morgan Stevens wasn't Dill's usual type. His brother had always gone for flashy women—bombshell blondes, busty brunettes and sassy redheads whose idea of keeping up with current events was to leaf through the tabloids while they had their hair styled. One of the dates Dill had brought to a family dinner last year had actually thought Austria was an abbreviation for Australia.

Morgan appeared to be intelligent and well-spoken, if her phone messages and letters were any indication. She was wearing conservative, if hideous, attire and, despite her advanced pregnancy, didn't appear to be built like a Playboy centerfold.

So, just what had Dill seen in this woman?

Bryan didn't have to wonder what Morgan had seen in Dill. His brother had been good-looking, charming and exceptionally free with his money, which he could afford to be since the money was actually Bryan's.

Gold digger.

It was an old-fashioned term, but Bryan had met enough of those sort of women over the years to know it still applied. Rock stars weren't the only ones who had groupies. Power brokers attracted them, too, though admittedly they were more refined and they tended to be looking for a ring and a Bergdorf charge card.

His ex-wife came to mind. She was remarried to a Texas oil tycoon whose fortune made the Caliborns' look paltry by comparison. And she'd borne the tycoon a son, a son who, for a brief time, she'd allowed Bryan to believe was his.

The scandal had been the talk of Chicago for months after the news broke. The DNA test results had been leaked to the media—even before Bryan had seen them. The gossipmongers had had a field day and they would again if they caught wind of this.

Morgan's moan brought him out of his bitter musings. Her lips parted and she began to pant. Her eyes were pinched closed, her face drawn and dotted with perspiration. She looked incredibly young and scared, especially when she whispered brokenly, "I don't…think I can…do this."

Bryan didn't like weakness. In business, he considered it a character flaw. Oddly, her vulnerability touched him. It made him want to go to her, hold her hand, stroke her cheek and offer reassurance. Absurd reactions, all. He folded his arms across his chest and leaned against the edge of his desk instead.

"Sure you can. You're going to be fine," the EMT told her. "Lie back on the couch now. I'm just going to check to see how far you've dilated."

That brought Bryan upright. He was no expert on labor and delivery, but he'd heard that term before and knew what it meant. On his way to the door, he said, "I'll be outside."

In the reception area, he paced uncharacteristically. He was used to taking charge of any given situation and then taking action. At the moment, he wasn't sure what to do. Should he call his folks, who were currently vacationing abroad, and tell them…what? What exactly could he say? Congratulations, you may soon be grandparents.

Dill's death had been so hard for Julia and Hugh Caliborn to accept. The death of a child, no matter how old, was wrong. It flouted the natural order of things. Parents were not supposed to bury their offspring.

Bryan pictured his mother upon hearing about Morgan's baby. She would be excited and weepy about reclaiming a precious bit of her younger son. No doubt, she would lavish the child with every comfort and amenity. And

Morgan, too, by default. She'd done the same with his former wife and the baby she'd been cruelly duped into believing was her first grandchild. Four months before the due date his mother had already made over one of her home's guest rooms into a nursery. Then she'd thrown her daughter-in-law a lavish shower, buying everything left on gift registry afterward. She'd been at the hospital for the birth, crying the happy tears women cry at such occasions. And, eighteen months later, when they'd learned that Caden Alexander Caliborn was not a Caliborn at all, she'd shed more tears, nearly as devastated as Bryan had been.

He clenched his fists. Until he knew for certain this young woman wasn't pulling a very convincing con, he had to protect them. That meant keeping news of Morgan not only from his parents, but from the press.

"Britney," he called as he stalked to her

desk. "Not a word of this leaves the building. If anyone in the conference room has questions about who this young woman is or why she came here looking for me today, you direct them to me. Understand?"

"Of course, Mr. Caliborn. You know you can count on me…for anything." Her smile was a just a little too personal for his liking, but he ignored it. In all other aspects, Britney was an efficient and loyal employee. Her apparent crush on him would wane in time, especially if he kept doing nothing to encourage it.

When he turned around, the EMTs were wheeling Morgan out of his office on the gurney. Her head was elevated. Her face was as white as a sheet.

"Will you be coming with us?" the older EMT asked. "We have room in the ambulance if you want to accompany your wife to the hospital."

Wife? He heard Britney gasp and gritted his teeth. Another rumor to dispel.

"She's not my wife," he bit out as the old bitterness returned. He glanced at his ring finger, recalling the gold band he'd once worn. To him, it had been a symbol of his love and fidelity. It wasn't until Camilla had asked for a divorce that he'd learned neither had been returned.

Whatever the EMT thought of Bryan's blunt denial, he masked with his professionalism. "Maybe you could make some calls for her then. It would be nice for her to have some support in labor and delivery, even if it doesn't look like she'll be in there long."

Bryan nodded and glanced at Morgan. In a gentler tone, he asked, "Who should I contact for you?"

Her eyes remained closed and though she was no longer panting; her voice was a breathy whisper when she replied, "No one."

"What about your family, your parents? Give me their number and I'll have Britney call them. They'll want to know."

Moisture had gathered at the corners of her closed eyes. It leaked down her temples now, blending into her perspiration-dampened hair. Weakness, he thought, once again drawn by her vulnerability. Before he realized what he was doing, he reached out and dried her tears.

Morgan's eyes flicked open at the contact. Green, he realized. A rich and vivid green. Like precious twin emeralds. He pulled back his hand and cleared his throat. "Your parents' number?"

"They're gone."

"Where can we reach them?" he asked.

"You can't." Bryan experienced an unfamiliar ache in his chest when Morgan whispered brokenly, "I have no one. No one at all."

CHAPTER TWO

SEVEN hours later, Bryan paced the length of the waiting room, sipping tepid coffee from a disposable cup while his gaze strayed to the large clock on the wall. It was after six, but Morgan remained in labor. So much for the EMT's assertion that the delivery would be accomplished quickly.

What was he doing at the hospital? He didn't have an exact answer, though duty ranked high on his list of choices. Given Morgan's claims, he felt a certain sense of obligation to follow up on the situation. Of course, that didn't explain why the minute the EMTs had wheeled her into the elevator he'd told Britney to clear his schedule for the afternoon, then he'd hopped in his Lexus, arriving at the hospital in record time. The entire way, he'd recalled Morgan's pinched features and heart-tugging vulnerability.

She needed someone. Bryan was the only someone available.

He finished the remainder of the coffee and tossed the cup into the receptacle. If he'd known the birth was going to take this long, he would have lingered at the office or at the very least brought his laptop with him. Duty, he thought again. As Windy City Industries' Vice President of Operations and soon to be CEO, he had plenty of work to keep him busy.

"Mr. Caliborn?"

He turned expectantly at the sound of the nurse's voice. The woman stood in the doorway, a smile lurking around her lips, which he took as a good sign. He hadn't realized he was holding his breath until she said, "The baby is a boy."

Another Caliborn boy. Was this one the real thing? He pushed aside that question and asked, "Is everything…okay?"

"Fine. The baby is perfectly healthy and a respectable seven pounds, eleven ounces."

He cleared his throat. "And Morgan?"

"She's doing well, all things considered. It was a difficult labor, especially toward the end. For a while the doctor thought he might have to take the baby by caesarean section, but it all worked out."

Because he didn't know what else to say— a rare occurrence for him and not an entirely pleasant one—he offered a curt nod. Then he went to collect his suit coat from the back of one of the chairs. If he hurried, he could catch a couple of members of his management team before they left their offices for the day and maybe go over some of the plans for the company's overseas expansion. But even as he was shoving his arm into a coat sleeve, he was changing his mind. Leaving seemed wrong.

"Excuse me!" he called out to stop the nurse. "I know it's late, but would it be possible for me to see…the baby?"

That's all he wanted, a glimpse at this child who might very well be his brother's legacy and the sole Caliborn heir, as Bryan certainly had no desire to put his heart on the line ever again. For him, marriage and fatherhood were a closed chapter.

"I think that can be arranged." The nurse smiled again before slipping out of the room.

Unfortunately, seeing the baby wasn't as simple as taking a quick peek in a nursery window so Bryan could assuage his curiosity while maintaining his distance. The newborn was with its mother, the nurse told him when, forty-five minutes later, she led him down the corridor to Morgan's room.

"Don't stay too long," she advised. "Morgan really needs her rest."

He raised his hand to knock. Even as his knuckles grazed the door he wondered what he would say. In a business setting he could hold his own, but he'd never been good at casual conversation with virtual strangers. That had been Dill's specialty.

After his knock, he waited for Morgan to call for him to come in. Instead, the door was flung wide by a bleary-eyed man decked out in wrinkled green scrubs and wearing a sappy grin.

"Have a cigar," the man said, thrusting a cellophane-wrapped stogie into Bryan's hand.

Bryan pegged him to be about thirty, and, given his attire, he'd been at the hospital for some time. So much for Morgan's Oscar-worthy claim that she had "no one." Disgusted with himself for falling once again for a woman's lies, he turned to leave.

"Hey, wait!" The man grabbed his arm. "I take it you're here to see the other new mom."

Other new mom? Bryan shifted back and glanced into the room. A brunette, presumably the man's wife, was holding a blanket-wrapped infant in the first bed. Beyond her, a drawn curtain partitioned the room.

"Maybe I should come back," Bryan said. He already felt awkward and now he was going to have an audience.

"Nah. Come in," the man coaxed, tugging on Bryan's arm. Lowering his voice, he added, "I think she could use some company. The nurses said she went through labor alone and I overheard them say she doesn't have a husband or anything." His cheeks turned red. "You're not the baby's—"

"No."

Bryan shook off the man's hand and walked to the far end of the room. When he peeked around the curtain, Morgan's eyes were closed. He used the opportunity to study her in a way that would have been rude if she were awake. Matted blond hair and a blotchy complexion offered proof of the hours she'd spent in labor…all alone. It wasn't guilt he felt. He had no reason for that. But something else nudged him. Admiration? She'd certainly shown a lot of grit when she'd burst into the conference room, demanding to see him. As she slept, her brow wrinkled and what he was experiencing shifted, softened. Once again he felt the odd desire to touch her and offer comfort.

From the other side of the curtain, he heard the man talking softly to his wife. Though Bryan couldn't hear the actual words, the tone was intimate. He recalled seeing a bouquet of fragrant flowers and a congratulatory helium balloon bobbing toward the ceiling. When Bryan's wife had given birth, he'd bought out the hospital's floral shop and had lavished her with gifts, including a diamond pendant necklace and matching earrings.

Morgan's side of the room was stark. No flowers, no balloons. No man whispering soft words of love and encouragement. No expensive gifts from a proud father. Bryan swallowed. He tried to picture Dill in the role of new dad. He tried to picture his brother being supportive and taking responsibility. But he couldn't. Even in a situation like this.

What was it Dillon had said upon learning Bryan was to become a father? After offering his congratulations, he'd added, "Better you than me."

How bitterly ironic.

From the bassinette beside the bed came a

faint sound, more like a mewling than a proper cry. Morgan might have been exhausted but her eyes opened immediately at the sound and a smile tugged at her lips.

"I'm here," she crooned softly as she shifted somewhat awkwardly to sit on the edge of the bed. "Mommy's here."

It was then that she noticed Bryan.

He cleared his throat, feeling as if he should apologize for intruding. Instead, he said, "Hello."

"Hi. I didn't realize you were here. I must have dozed off for a minute." She attempted to run her fingers through her hair, only to have them snag in a knotted clump of pale gold. Her cheeks grew pink.

"I won't stay. If I'd known you were asleep…" He shrugged. "I just stopped in to see the baby and… Do you need anything?"

"No." Then she shrugged. "Well, the little

suitcase I had packed and ready for the hospital would be nice. I have a hairbrush in it, among other things." Her smile turned wry.

"Where is it? I'll send someone for it."

"At my hotel." When she mentioned the hotel's name Bryan's lips must have twisted in distaste, because she said dryly, "Apparently it's not up to your high standards."

No, it wasn't. The place was little more than a flophouse. He kept that opinion to himself, though the idea of her and the baby—of any young, single woman and helpless infant—staying there bothered him tremendously.

"I'll have Britney bring it by first thing in the morning."

"Thank you." When he backed up a step, she said, "Don't you want a closer look?"

He did. That was why he'd come to her room when good sense had told him to be on his way. Yet he hesitated, oddly more afraid of what he might *not* see than what he might.

The baby was lying on its back. Bryan remembered from Caden's infancy that doctors recommended the position to prevent Sudden Infant Death Syndrome. When Caden had learned to roll over onto his stomach, Bryan had woken up at all hours of the night to check on him, watching his tiny back rise and fall in the low light of the nursery.

"He has hair under the cap," Morgan said.

Bryan spied a few dark brown wisps poking out. Puffy eyes, that deep sea-blue ubiquitous to newborns, were wide open, and though the baby probably was merely trying to focus, he seemed to be regarding Bryan. Finally, one side of his tiny mouth crooked up in a fair imitation of a smile.

Dillon.

Bryan felt as if he'd taken a sledgehammer

to the solar plexus. He saw his brother in that little face, not in obvious ways, for the baby's features were too small. But taken in total, they reflected familiarity. Bryan's heart ached again, this pain bittersweet because he couldn't be completely sure he was seeing things as they were or as he wished them to be.

That had been the case once before. And how it had cost him to believe and later find out he'd been deceived.

"What will you name him?" he asked stiffly.

"Brice Dillon Stevens."

He nodded, not surprised that she'd worked his brother's name in somehow. But he wondered if Morgan had chosen to give the child her surname because she was unmarried or because she knew the baby wasn't really a Caliborn. Of course, that hadn't stopped Bryan's ex-wife. She'd tossed the child's paternity in his face when their marriage had splintered apart. She'd stayed with Bryan for all the months it took her to convince the oil tycoon he was the biological father.

Bryan's lips twisted at the memory.

"I suppose you listed my brother as the father on the birth certificate?"

"I did. Is that a problem for you?" Morgan's voice held an edge that belied her otherwise fragile appearance. She looked so young and vulnerable in that hideous hospital-issue gown that snapped closed at the shoulders. Yet her direct gaze and even more direct query hinted at steel.

He ignored her question. "I'll be going. You need your rest." Before he did, though, he removed a business card from his wallet and handed it to her. "If you require anything else, my private number is on the back."

"Thanks, but I won't be calling. I'm…" She glanced down at the baby, her expression softening in a way that tugged at him. "*We're going to be just fine.*"

After Bryan's departure the doubts Morgan had been experiencing for the past several months once again began circling like vultures, picking away at her usual optimism and determination.

We're going to be just fine.

Were they?

What had she been thinking, packing up and crossing state lines without a firm plan in place? That wasn't like her. Of course, nothing about her current situation fell within her personal range of normal. What was she going to do for a job, a place to live?

She hadn't come to Chicago expecting Bryan—er, Dillon—to help out financially, though their child certainly was entitled legally and morally to monetary support. But she had hoped he would offer to pitch in on some expenses, such as the hospital bill. After that, she'd planned to leave up to him how much or how little he wanted to be involved in his son's life both physically and financially. Morgan wasn't a charity case. She had a small settlement from her parents' estate. Unfortunately, the higher cost of living in Chicago was chewing through it more quickly than she'd anticipated.

And now she'd discovered that Dillon not only had lied to her about his identity, but he had been killed in an accident every bit as unforeseeable as the one that had claimed her parents. Gazing at the son they had created together in Aruba, she wasn't quite sure how to feel. Being angry over his betrayal served no purpose. He was gone. She wanted to mourn the man she had known as Bryan, and she did, in the abstract way one mourns any life that is snatched away too soon. And, of course, she mourned him as her baby's father. Morgan had been lucky enough to enjoy a close relationship with both of her parents, but she'd been especially tight with her dad. She'd wanted the same for Brice. God knew her son had precious few relatives as it was, with her parents gone.

As for mourning Dillon as someone significant to her, she didn't. She couldn't. It simply wasn't possible since she hadn't known him well. Indeed, beyond physically, she hadn't known him at all, she realized again, and experienced another wave of shame. She wasn't the sort of woman who engaged in a vacation fling, which perhaps explained why she'd gotten pregnant the one and only time she'd been foolish enough to throw caution to the wind. Or maybe subconsciously she had wanted a child, someone to love and nurture and to help fill up the yawning emptiness she'd felt since her parents' deaths.

Whatever the reason, looking at her newborn son now she had no regrets.

"I love you," she whispered, leaning over to stroke his cheek.

Indeed, Morgan had loved him from the time she'd learned he was growing inside her. But love, even a love this grand and expansive, wasn't capable of obliterating her concerns. And she had plenty of those.

From the other side of the curtain, she could hear the couple discussing who they wanted to act as their newborn's godparents. Judging from the number of names they tossed around, they had a lot of people to choose from. Morgan wasn't completely without relatives, though none lived in the midwest. She did have a small circle of friends back in Wisconsin. A couple of them had urged her to stay in town even after she'd lost her job.

Jen Woolworth, another teacher, one with more seniority who had weathered the latest round of cuts, had been particularly vocal against Morgan leaving the state.

"Hon, you're due soon. You shouldn't be traveling, let alone moving. Stay here with us," she'd urged.

The offer had been tempting. Jen was a dear friend and the two of them often grabbed a cup of coffee after school or hooked up on the weekends for a little shopping and girl talk. But Jen shared a small bungalow-style home with her husband, two rambunctious prepubescent boys and an incontinent miniature poodle they had named Puddles for obvious reasons.

They had enough chaos and no room for another adult, let alone an adult and an infant, even if Jen claimed it would be no big deal to make her boys bunk together in one of the small bedrooms, freeing up the other ten-by-eleven-foot space to serve as Morgan's living quarters and nursery.

The baby fussed. Morgan pulled down her gown, recalling the instructions she'd received in her prenatal classes. Nursing should have been easy. It was the most natural thing in the world, right? But Brice seemed as baffled by it as she was, and he grew fussier by the minute. Finally, he all-out wailed. It was a pitiful sound, heartbreaking. As tears brimmed in Morgan's eyes, she felt demoralized.

We're going to be fine.

The words mocked her now. Had she really said them to Bryan less than half an hour ago? Had she, even for a moment, really believed it herself?

She wanted to join Brice in crying, but she

didn't. She'd never been a quitter and she wasn't about to become one now. Her son needed her. He was depending on her. She couldn't let him down. The luxury of tears would have to wait.

"Let's try this again," she murmured resolutely.

He finally latched on after a couple more false starts.

The flowers—a huge vase full of festive daisies, lilies and delicate irises—arrived as Morgan was putting Brice back in the bassinet. She couldn't imagine who would have sent her such an expensive bouquet. No one back in Wisconsin knew Morgan had given birth and she didn't know anyone in Chicago. Well, no one except for… No way.

She plucked the little white envelope from its holder among the blooms and tore it open. Sure enough, written in slashing bold cursive under the card's pre-printed congratulatory message was the name *Bryan Caliborn*.

The *real* Bryan Caliborn.

She blinked. Who would have guessed that hard, brooding man could be so thoughtful? An hour later, when a couple of orderlies came to move her and the baby to a private room down the hall, Morgan added the word *accommodating* to his attributes. This room was far more spacious and included amenities such as a plush rocking chair, cable television, a padded window seat and framed reproductions of museum-quality art on the walls.

Just about the time Morgan was beginning to think she'd completely misjudged him, Bryan ruined it with his edict.

That's what the typewritten missive amounted to. It was delivered the morning she was to be released from the hospital by the same snooty receptionist who'd brought

Morgan's suitcase by the day before: Britney. The young woman arrived just as Morgan finished dressing in a shapeless, oversize dress. Of course, Britney looked slender and runway chic in a fitted jacket, flirty skirt and peep-toe high heels.

"This is for you." Britney set a large shopping bag on the bed and handed Morgan a note. It was from his highness.

Though Morgan was curious about the contents of the bag, she was even more so about the note.

Morgan,
I have sent a car to deliver you and the baby to new accommodations that you may use for the rest of your stay in Chicago. Your bill at the hotel has been settled in full and I've taken the liberty of having your belongings collected and moved.

I have asked Britney to accompany you.
I will be in contact later this evening to en-
sure you have everything you need.

Bryan

Relief came first. This was the answer to
her prayers. Just the thought of taking Brice
to that dingy hotel room that reeked of stale
cigarette smoke made her nauseated. And
housekeeping and laundry services were
included. What new mother wouldn't appreciate help with those time-consuming chores?
But Bryan's motive puzzled her. Was he
doing this because he believed her or was he
merely interested in keeping a closer eye on
her? She read the note again, but still was
unable to decipher any clues. This time,
however, relief wasn't all she felt. It chafed
her pride that he'd made the arrangements
and moved her things without at least running

his plan by her first. She didn't like being told what to do.

Nor what to wear, she added, when Britney scooted the bag closer and said, "Mr. Caliborn told me to pick up an outfit suitable for your trip home from the hospital."

"I have clothes," Morgan objected.

Britney eyed her dubiously before going on. "Yes, well, I brought a couple of selections for you to choose from. I had to guess your size, but I went with loose-fitting styles," she added, her gaze straying to Morgan's midsection.

Morgan knew she still looked pregnant. Not the ready-to-pop balloon she'd appeared to be at her first encounter with the svelte Britney, but a good four or five months gone.

"I have clothes," she said a second time. The words came out forcefully, causing the baby to rouse from his slumber.

"Mr. Caliborn felt you would be more comfortable in fresh things," Britney clarified.

"You can tell Mr. Caliborn—" Morgan began, fully intending to decline the offer, but that was as far as she got before Britney pulled a subtly printed dress from the bag. Then Morgan's only concern was, "God, I hope that fits."

Britney's brows arched. "I can tell Mr. Caliborn what?"

"That I said thank you. And that I will reimburse him."

It did fit. Morgan had to hand it to Britney. The woman not only had a good eye for fashion, she had a good eye for what would look best on Morgan's post-pregnancy body. While nothing could completely camouflage her tummy, the dress Britney had picked certainly minimized it, while accentuating a couple of assets that also had been enhanced by pregnancy. She just hoped Brice wouldn't need to nurse between now and the time they reached wherever it was they were going, because the dress, which zipped in the back, wasn't made for that function.

"Much better," Britney said when she saw Morgan.

Her tone bordered on astonished, but it was hard for Morgan to be offended when she agreed.

"Thank you."

With a curt nod, Britney glanced at her watch. "I've called for an orderly to bring a wheelchair. You've signed your discharge papers, right?"

"I did that before you arrived."

She nodded again and pulled out her cell phone. "Noah, it's Britney. Have the car waiting at the main entrance in fifteen minutes."

Morgan might have felt a bit like Cinderella then, except Britney was hardly fairy-godmother material and, of course, she had no Prince Charming.

Then Britney said into the phone, "If you see any photographers, call me back immediately and we'll go to plan B."

"Photographers?" Morgan asked as soon as the other woman hung up.

"Paparazzi. Every effort has been made to keep news of you and your son under wraps, but it pays to be cautious."

"I'm afraid I still don't understand."

Britney huffed out a breath. "The Caliborns are a big deal in this city. They're in the headlines regularly for business and philanthropic reasons, but scandals always sell more papers than straight news."

Great. Morgan was a scandal, her son's birth fodder for the tabloids. No wonder Bryan had been eager to find her "alternative accommodations."

CHAPTER THREE

MORGAN stepped into the apartment foyer behind Britney and gasped. She certainly hadn't expected her new place to be a penthouse that offered views of Lake Michigan and the famous Navy Pier from windows that ran the length of the exterior wall.

In the large living room the color scheme was heavy on beige and other neutrals with nary a punch of color. The furniture was tasteful and obviously top quality, and included a baby grand piano that had Morgan's fingertips tingling to play just looking at it, but the place didn't look lived-in. Indeed, every last inch of it seemed as cold as the foyer's Italian marble floor.

"Who owns this place?" Morgan asked. She swore the question echoed.

"Mr. Caliborn. It's his home," Britney replied with a roll of her eyes.

"He lives here?" That came as a surprise. He had such an imposing personality she'd expected to see it stamped on his belongings.

"Since his divorce three years ago." The secretary arched a brow then and asked sarcastically, "What? It's not up to *your* standards?"

"It's not that. It just seems a little…impersonal." Yes, that was the word. It looked more like a showroom in a high-end furniture store than a home. "There aren't even any photographs."

"Mr. Caliborn isn't the sentimental sort."

Morgan wasn't sure she agreed. He kept a picture of Dillon in his office. And she also recalled seeing one of an older couple, most likely his parents. And then there were the flowers he'd sent to her hospital room. She said as much to Britney.

"Don't be so naive, Miss Stevens. Appearances are important to someone in his position. Precautions have been taken just in case the press ever gets wind of you and your…situation. Hence the flowers." Her gaze lowered. "And the new frock he had me select in case some industrious photographer managed to snap a shot of you leaving the hospital. Think of it as damage control."

Damage control? Morgan felt as if she'd been doused in ice water, yet for all that she was steaming mad. Before she could muster a response, though, Britney was moving past her, high heels clicking purposefully on the marble floor before she disappeared through an arched doorway off the living room.

Morgan was left with little choice but to trail behind her. After passing through the formal dining room, Morgan caught up with Britney in the kitchen.

"The pantry is fully stocked and so is the refrigerator." The young woman opened the stainless-steel behemoth's double doors, revealing shelves lined with staples including milk, juice, cheese, eggs and butter. The crispers were bursting with a mouth-watering assortment of fresh fruits and vegetables. "Mr. Caliborn said to help yourself and to make a list of anything else you need. He has a housekeeper who comes in twice a week to do the cleaning and laundry. Hilda also takes care of buying his groceries."

So he'd mentioned in his note. But that brought up a most pertinent question. "Where will Mr. Caliborn be staying?"

"His parents are abroad for the summer. He's

moved to their residence in Lake Forest for the time being." Britney cast Morgan a quelling look. "It means he'll have a longer commute to work, but apparently he felt you would be more comfortable here than in a hotel."

Some of Morgan's anger dissipated. She *would* be more comfortable here. That went without saying, but Morgan didn't want to displace Bryan from his home and disrupt his routine. She would call him after Britney left. Maybe they could come up with a different solution.

"Besides, the doorman here is vigilant in guarding Mr. Caliborn's privacy, and as such he'll be sure to keep any reporters from slipping up to see you."

Ah, yes. Damage control.

Brice stirred in her arms then. She lifted him to her shoulder and pulled off the little cap he was wearing. Dropping a kiss on his crown, she murmured, "Hey, sleepyhead, are you finally waking up?"

Britney's gaze shifted to the baby. She was a career woman, emphasis on *career*, but surely she wasn't immune to the allure of a newborn. Rather than softening, however, her expression hardened. Apparently, she was.

Still, Morgan asked, "Would you like to have children someday?"

Britney wrinkled her nose. "God, no! Though I suppose *accidentally* getting pregnant can wind up being the ticket to the good life."

Morgan felt sucker punched. "What do you mean by that?"

The other woman snorted. "Take a look around and you'll figure it out."

"You think I'm after money?"

"Yes," Britney said baldly. "And I doubt I'm the only one to reach that conclusion. I suggest you don't get too comfortable with the

Caliborn lifestyle. Bryan's noble sense of obligation aside, ultimately, you're not his type."

Two things occurred to Morgan then. First,
Britney didn't know that the baby was
Dillon's, and second, the young woman had a
serious crush on her boss.

Well, Morgan wasn't going to clarify the
situation if Bryan hadn't. Though she
longed to assure Britney the brooding businessman wasn't her type either, she kept her
mouth closed.

"The bedrooms are this way." Britney click-
clacked out of the kitchen, once again leaving
Morgan to follow in her wake. "The one at the
end of the hall is Mr. Caliborn's. You'll be
using the guest suite."

Britney swung open the first door they came
to, revealing a large and neatly furnished
room. The queen-size bed was outfitted in a
taupe duvet. The walls were a couple of

shades darker in the same color. A crib, changing table and glider-rocker were set up against the far wall. The pastel-blue bumper pads and comforter provided the only color.

Before Morgan could ask about the nursery furniture, Britney said, "Mr. Caliborn ordered furnishings for the baby. They're top-of-the-line, of course."

"But I have a crib and changing table." They'd belonged to her friend Jen, who had given them to Morgan as a shower gift. For the time being they were in storage with the rest of her belongings.

Britney shrugged. "Now you have two. You'll find diapers, wipes and all that sort of thing in the drawers of the changing table."

"He's thought of everything," Morgan murmured, finding it impossible not to be touched by his efforts, no matter what their motivation.

"Yes. He always does." Britney glanced at her watch, clearly eager to be gone. "My cell phone number is programmed into the telephone. You may call me at any time."

"Oh, that's not necessary."

"Mr. Caliborn thinks it is." With that, Britney left.

Mr. Caliborn thinks…

Mr. Caliborn feels…

Mr. Caliborn has decided…

Under other circumstances, Morgan would have screamed. But as irritatingly high-handed as he could be and as independent as she'd always been, the fact was, she needed someone and he was the only someone available. As she laid Bricc down in the brand-new crib in a room that smelled of fresh linens she couldn't help but be grateful they were not back in the claustrophobic hotel room breathing tainted air.

As soon as she could manage it, she would

find a job and another place to live. In the meantime, she would suck up her pride and do what was best for her son.

The knock on the door surprised her. It was after eight o'clock that night and Morgan was curled up on the living room couch. The television was on, though she wasn't really watching it. She had too much on her mind to follow the sitcom's quick-paced dialogue.

Britney's confidence in the doorman's abilities aside, Morgan checked the peephole before flipping open the dead bolt. A grim-looking Bryan stood in the hallway, arms folded across his broad chest.

"Hello," she said after opening the door.

Dark eyes surveyed her, no doubt taking in the oversize shirt and unflattering sweatpants. "I hope this isn't a bad time. I forgot my shaving kit when I packed up my things earlier."

"Oh. Sure. Come in." She stepped back to allow him entry.

"The baby sleeping?"

"For the time being," she said wryly. If she got lucky, she would have another hour before Brice roused and demanded to be fed.

Bryan nodded. "Britney said she showed you around. I take it everything is to your liking."

"Yes." She laced her fingers together. "She mentioned that you're staying at your parents' home in Lake Forest and that they are out of the country."

"They keep a villa in the south of France. Now that my father is getting closer to retirement, they've been spending large blocks of time there," he said matter-of-factly, as if everyone's folks had a second home on the French Riviera.

She pictured the elder Caliborns, pampered, snobbish and every bit as laconic and dictatorial as their eldest son. Heaven help her. Morgan had wanted Brice to have extended family, loving relatives to help fill in the gaps a single mother couldn't. Now she wasn't so sure she would be doing him any favors.

Still, she said, "I had hoped to meet them and to have them get to know Brice. He is their grandson, after all."

"Perhaps on another visit to Chicago," he suggested with a shrug.

She didn't bother to correct his assumption that she was just visiting. It was fast becoming apparent that moving here had been a huge mistake, even if she still felt strongly that she should live in closer proximity to the only family her child had.

"They don't know about me," she guessed.

"No."

"And you're not planning to tell them."

"Not yet."

No need to ask what he was waiting for. Obviously, he required proof of Brice's parentage. She expected him to request a paternity test then. When he didn't, Morgan decided to change the subject.

"I want to reimburse you for the groceries and, of course, for the amount you've had to spend on damage control."

Dark brows tugged together. "Pardon?"

"The bouquet of flowers, the private room and the new dress purchased for me to wear home from the hospital," she clarified. "Britney mentioned that the baby and I would make excellent tabloid fodder and, as such, appearances had to be maintained."

Bryan scowled, but he didn't deny it. Instead, he said, "No reimbursement is necessary. I wanted you to have those things."

"Well, I insist on paying for my lodgings. When you get right down to it, I'm subletting your apartment." She swallowed, knowing a Chicago penthouse with this incredible view and a rooftop patio far exceeded her limited budget, but she wasn't going to stay here long and pride wouldn't allow her to freeload, especially since Bryan clearly expected her to do just that. "If you'll have a contract drawn up, I'll pay the full rent and utilities for the next month."

"I own it."

Of course he did. "Then, whatever you feel is fair."

"When the month is up, will you be returning to—Cherry Bluff, Wisconsin, isn't it?"

"No, I don't think I'll be going back." Other than her friends, there was nothing for Morgan there. As much as she missed Jen, she could no more freeload off her than she could off Bryan.

"What about your job?"

"I lost it."

"I see." Almost instantly, his dark eyes lit with speculation, suspicion.

Both stung. "I wasn't fired. I was pink-slipped."

"Another word for the same thing, I believe."

"Not from my point of view. I loved my job and I was good at it. The principal hated to see me go, but the school district had to make cuts." She folded her arms. "Perhaps you've noticed that the economy isn't as strong as it once was. Well, in bad times, the arts are the first thing to face the ax."

He appeared surprised. "You're a teacher?"

"A music teacher, yes." She nodded her head in the direction of the baby grand. Her own upright was sitting in storage. "You have a lovely piano. Do you play?"

"Not really."

"Oh." It seemed a waste for an instrument like that to go unused.

He apparently read her mind. "I assume that you do." When she nodded, he said, "Feel free to use it, although it probably needs a good tuning."

"If it does, I'll pay for it."

He sighed, shook his head. Was that amusement she spied in his gaze or exasperation? "Fine, but I'll hear no more talk about contracts and subletting. That subject is closed."

Morgan didn't argue. When she moved out, she would leave a check to cover her expenses. Bryan Caliborn would discover she could be every bit as stubborn as he was. Still, she had to know, "Are you still worried about appearances just in case I'm found out?"

"Among other things," he answered evasively. The enigmatic response as well as the way he was watching her made her wonder what those other things might be.

"Well, for the record, I do appreciate your

kindness, even if I feel funny about taking over your home."

"Don't."

One word uttered resolutely. Another edict. It grated against her already raw pride. "You know, you have a very annoying habit of telling me what to do and, now, what to think."

A pair of dark brows shot up, telling her she wasn't the only one who was annoyed. No doubt he wasn't used to being talked to in such a manner. She waited for a blistering retort. Instead, he bowed mockingly.

"My apologies."

Damn him! He was humoring her. "I'd accept them if I thought they were sincere."

"You're questioning my sincerity?"

In her stocking feet Morgan was a full head shorter than Bryan. Even so, she squared her shoulders and raised her chin. "Yes, I am."

"God, you're so damned—" he was frowning when he finished with "—refreshing."

The description threw her, as did the momentary confusion she'd glimpsed in his eyes. "I don't know what to make of that," she replied honestly.

He snorted out a laugh. "Good. We're even then, because I don't know what to make of you."

And he didn't. Bryan usually could read people easily enough. Morgan, however, remained an enigma despite her blunt talk. Interestingly, the more time he spent with her, the more baffled he became. And the more curious. With that in mind, he said, "I'll just get my shaving kit and be on my way."

When Bryan returned to the living room, she was seated at the piano playing softly in deference to the infant sleeping down the hall. In the room's low light, she looked almost ethereal, though the sound emanating from the piano was anything but heavenly. Even to his untrained ears he could tell it was off-key.

"How bad is it?"

She glanced up. "Abysmal. It's a crime what you've allowed to happen to an instrument of this quality."

He nearly smiled at her damning words. She certainly wasn't one to pull punches. "I'd apologize, but I'm pretty sure you'd only accuse me of being insincere again."

"You're mocking me." She plunked out more of the discordant melody.

"Only a little."

She wasn't amused. "I find that almost as intolerable as the fact that you don't trust me and yet feel the need to clothe and shelter me as if I'm some sort of helpless waif."

"Oh, I wouldn't call you helpless. I'd say you've managed quite nicely up till now."

Her eyes widened at the jab.

"Stop it! Just stop it!" she shouted, looking angry and exhausted enough to make him feel petty. "I don't know what your problem is, but it's *your* problem. Not mine. I'm not after the precious Caliborn fortune."

"If I had a dime for every time a woman has said that—"

She slammed the lid down over the piano keys. "And to think I was starting to feel grateful for all of your help. I'd get Brice and leave right now if my car wasn't still parked across town in your company's lot."

He knew he'd regret it later, but he couldn't stop himself from adding, "And if you had someplace to go. But you don't, Morgan. No place to go and no job. Which is why you came to Chicago."

Her eyes turned bright. Her voice became hoarse. "How is it possible that you and

Dillon were brothers? I've asked you for nothing. You're the one who insisted on moving me into your apartment, yet you're so suspicious."

I have good reason to be, he thought, calling on bitter memories to make him immune to her tears. He wouldn't be played for a sucker a second time.

"You're right, Morgan. Dill and I are very different men. You'd do well to remember that." He lowered his voice to a more intimate level and added, "Although I can assure you there are certain things I am every bit as skilled at as you found my brother to be."

She shot to her feet, shaking with justified outrage as she poked a finger in the direction of the door. "Out! Get out of here right now!"

Bryan didn't question her right to order him from his own home. He did as she asked, already hating himself for the cheap shot and not at all sure why he'd taken it.

Bryan sat at his desk staring sightlessly out at the Chicago skyline as he levered a gold fountain pen between his fingers. He was too keyed up to concentrate on work, though he had plenty of it to occupy his attention. His agitation had nothing to do with the fact that Windy City's last quarter's earnings were not what he'd hoped they would be. He was thinking about Morgan.

It had been almost a month since he'd last seen or spoken with her. And though part of him knew he owed her an apology for the unforgivable comment he'd made, he couldn't force himself to do so. In fact, just yesterday, after uncharacteristic foot-dragging, he'd hired a private investigator to probe her past. It was time to find out a little more about

Morgan Stevens than what could be gleaned at face value. It wasn't just that he couldn't bring himself to trust her, though that was part of it. He didn't trust himself and this odd desire he had to believe she was exactly what she claimed to be.

Now she'd thrown him for a loop again. She'd called half an hour ago and left a message with Britney that she would be moving out of the penthouse later that day.

That didn't make sense. Nor did the fact that even though Bryan had a meeting with his management team in forty-five minutes, he was pushing himself away from his desk and preparing to stride out of his office. He needed to get to the bottom of this.

When he arrived at the apartment door twenty minutes later, he didn't knock. He let himself in only to stumble over the luggage that was stacked in the foyer. She was packed and ready to go. But she was leaving a bit of herself behind, he noticed. His beige sofa now sported a pair of plump red pillows, and a throw of the same hue was tossed over the chair. Three weeks in his home and she'd infused it with more vibrancy and life than he'd managed in three years. But then, this was just a place for him to lay his head at night. He'd stopped wanting a home the day he'd learned he didn't really have a son.

On the coffee table he spied an envelope with his name on it. He opened it to find a check made out to him. The sum had him shaking his head. She was either a clever actress or had too much pride for her own good. Though it wasn't large by his standards, it was probably far more than Morgan could afford. With an oath, he tore it in half before stuffing it into his pocket.

From down the hallway came an infant's

shrill cries. He followed the sound, stopping outside the open door to the guest suite. Morgan was at the changing table with her back to him. She'd lost weight. That much was obvious despite the oversize clothing she wore. Her hair was pulled into a ponytail that made her look deceptively young. She was talking in soothing tones as she put a fresh diaper on the screaming baby.

"Hey, hey. Come on now, Brice. It's not as bad as all that," she said. "We're going to be fine, you and me. We're a team, remember?"

The baby quieted, almost as if he understood. More likely, though, the reason was because his bottom was dry and he was being lifted into the security of his mother's arms. The baby eyed Bryan over her shoulder. Brice had more hair now. It stood up on end at the crown. And he'd acquired another chin. He and Morgan made quite a picture, the perfect snapshot of everything Bryan had held dear.

Before learning it was a lie.

He cleared his throat. Upon hearing the sound, she whirled around. The warmth that had been in her tone when she'd spoken to Brice was absent when she told Bryan, "I'll be out in less than an hour."

"It's hardly necessary for you to leave."

"I think it is," she replied.

"Where are you going?"

"Does it matter?"

It did—for reasons he couldn't explain to himself, much less to her. He should be happy she was going. Glad to be rid of her. Except…

"Look, Morgan, I want to apologize. What I said to you the last time I was here, it was…crude."

"Insufferably so," she agreed with a nod. "But your appalling lack of manners is not the reason I'm leaving. My plan was to stay here until I found employment, and I have."

This came as a surprise. "You've been looking for a job?"

She rolled her eyes. "I know you'll find this hard to believe, but I've always been self-sufficient and I prefer to remain that way."

"What kind of job?"

"I'll be turning tricks in the blue-light district. I hear I can set my own hours," she deadpanned. "A teaching job, of course."

"Were you called back to the school in Wisconsin then?" Oddly, his stomach clenched as he awaited her reply.

"No. I'll be staying in Chicago, at least for the time being."

He ignored the relief that had him wanting to sigh, perhaps because a new worry surfaced.

"Which school will you teach at?" Some of the public ones could be kind of rough.

Though he admired Morgan's spunk, it made his blood run cold to think of her going toe-to-toe with some young gang recruit.

"Actually, I won't be in a school." She lifted her chin. "I've been hired by a south-side community center to give lessons as part of an after-school program that's being funded through a Tempest Herriman Foundation grant."

His eyes narrowed. "That doesn't sound long-term or, for that matter, very lucrative. Is it even going to cover your expenses?"

"I don't see how that's your concern," Morgan snapped irritably.

He shrugged. And though it was far from the truth, he reminded her, "Appearances."

"Appearances!" she spat. "If I wasn't holding Brice right now, I'd describe to you, in minute detail, what you can do with your appearances."

"Please, don't hold back. He's too young to

grasp words. It's tone that babies this age understand."

"Now you're an expert on children?" She expelled a breath, but then continued in a voice suited to a nursery rhyme, "Maybe it's a good thing you don't believe he's a Caliborn. I don't want my son raised around someone as superficial and self-important as you are."

Bryan ignored the insults. He was a firm believer in quid pro quo, so he figured she was entitled to fling them. Besides, she looked absolutely lovely, with her color high and those emerald eyes flashing in dangerous fashion as she put him in his place.

Stepping fully into the room, he commented conversationally, "I never would have taken you to be the sort to cut off your nose to spite your face."

"That's not what I'm doing."

"No? You're going to move your son, who's

barely a month old, out of the safety and comfort of my penthouse and take a job on the city's south side making peanuts. What about health insurance?"

Morgan said nothing, but she swallowed hard and he had his answer.

"No benefits," he scoffed with a shake of his head and then drew closer. "And where are you going to live, Morgan? In some fleabag apartment on a par with that hotel where you were staying before the baby was born? Be reasonable."

"Being reasonable hasn't gotten me very far with you." She abandoned the sweet tone. "You've done your level best to make me feel unwelcome, yet now you have the audacity to act amazed that I'm leaving. What do you want from me? Just what do you want?"

She'd shouted the last question and now the baby began to wail. She looked on the verge of losing it herself. That had him panicked, both because he knew Morgan's tears were the real thing and because the bullying he typically reserved for the boardroom was the primary cause.

"God, don't cry."

"Don't tell me what to do," she countered on a sob. "I've had it up to here with your edicts. I've had it up to here with you. Go away, Bryan. Just go away."

He ignored the directive. In fact, he stepped closer. Close enough that he could smell the scent of baby powder. Close enough that he could have run his knuckles along the underside of her quivering jaw if he'd wanted to. And, God help him, he wanted to.

"Stay, Morgan. Not for the sake of appearances."

"Why then?"

Because I want you to, he thought. I want to

get to know you, figure you out. How nonsensical was that? So, he said, "Because it's the right thing to do for Brice."

The fight went out of her. Her shoulders slumped and she lowered her chin. Bryan leaned closer until her forehead was resting on his chest. Brice quieted, too, cocooned between them.

After a moment she sighed. "That's so low."

He laughed without humor. "Yes, but we've already established that I'm a bastard."

She lifted her head and, without heat, admonished, "Don't swear in front of the baby."

"Sorry."

"I'll stay, but only until your parents return. They still don't know about Brice, do they?"

"No."

She shook her head. "Why am I not surprised?"

"They've been through so much pain." The

loss of what they believed to be their first grandchild as well as the death of their younger son.

"And you're sure I'll cause them more," she said sadly.

He stepped back, turned away. "I have reasons for being the way that I am," he said slowly. It was as much of an explanation as he could bring himself to give her and more of one than he would have offered anyone else.

"Well, unless you want to live a very lonely life, you're going to have to get over those reasons."

CHAPTER FOUR

BRYAN sat across from his date in the upscale French restaurant, sipping a nice pinot noir and pretending to listen to his date while he replayed the conversation he'd had with Morgan that day three weeks earlier in his apartment.

…unless you want to live a very lonely life, you're going to have to get over those reasons.

She was wrong. He wasn't lonely, he assured himself. Far from it.

"Don't you agree?" Courtney said now.

"Of course," he replied, nodding even though he hadn't a clue as to what had just been said.

All he knew was he had *exactly* what he wanted. Courtney Banks was worldly and wealthy and, okay, every bit as cynical as he was when it came to members of the opposite sex thanks to her own ugly divorce. But that made her perfect. She had absolutely no interest in settling down a second time and absolutely no need for his money. Since not long after his divorce, she and Bryan had gotten together whenever either of them felt the need for a no-strings-attached evening of fun. That's why he'd called her tonight, but now the only woman on his mind was an outspoken blonde about whom he had no business thinking, much less dreaming as he had last night.

"You're not listening," Courtney accused, laughing.

Blinking, he said, "Excuse me?"

"You just agreed with me that the White Sox are a far superior ball club to the Cubs, and we both know what a rabid Cubs fan you are."

He winced. "Sorry. I guess I have a lot on my mind tonight."

"If I didn't know better, Bryan, I might find myself jealous."

He reached across the table and squeezed her hand. "You're not the jealous type." Not to mention the fact that nothing about their relationship warranted the emotion. They weren't exclusive. They weren't committed. Neither one of them had spouted words of love, because, quite frankly, neither one of them wanted to fall in love again.

Courtney's shoulders lifted in a delicate shrug. "I may not be jealous, but I am greedy. When I'm with a man, I want to be the only thing on his mind."

"That's no less than you deserve," he agreed. And more than he was capable of this night. "Would you hate me if we ended the evening early? I'm not fit company."

"*Hate* is the wrong word. I'll be disappointed, though, and so will you. I had plans to model new lingerie." She sent him a smile that in the past had sent blood pumping through his veins. He waited, hoping it would this time, but it had no effect on him.

"It's my loss," he said graciously.

"Yes, it is, and I'm glad you understand that." Her brows rose meaningfully.

He paid the bill and they left the restaurant. After he dropped Courtney off at her Lake Shore Drive address, he should have continued north on 41 to Lake Forest, but Bryan found himself driving south instead. Back into the city. To his penthouse and Morgan.

It was past nine when he arrived at the door. He hesitated before knocking, oddly nervous. Maybe he should have called first. Hell, he shouldn't even be here. What was he thinking? Even as he asked himself this, he raised his fist and rapped three times. If she didn't answer right away, he would go.

The door swung open a moment later. Morgan was dressed in jeans and a T-shirt that she'd left untucked. Her feet were bare, her toenails painted a sheer pink. She'd pulled her hair into a messy ponytail that was a nod to necessity rather than style. Other than a faint sheen of gloss on her lips, her face was free of makeup.

Bryan wasn't sure what to make of the intense awareness that had him sucking in a breath. He only knew it didn't bode well for him.

"This is a surprise," she said.

"It's late and I should have called first," he replied, echoing his earlier thoughts. "Sorry."

"That's okay. I'm up."

"I wanted to pick up a few shirts." Which was a complete lie. "Mind if I come in?"

"It's your home." She shrugged and stepped

back. "Don't tell me you're just getting off work."

"No. I was…out with a friend for dinner."

Her brows rose at the same time her lips twitched. "Is that code for a date?"

He didn't know whether to laugh or sigh. She saved him the trouble of having to decide by asking, "Can I take your coat or won't you be staying that long?"

He shrugged out of his suit jacket by way of an answer and handed it to her. While she hung it in the foyer closet, he reached up to loosen his tie. He was unbuttoning his collar when she turned. She averted her gaze.

"Am I making you uncomfortable?"

"No. Well, not as long as you stop with that button," she said bluntly.

"That was the plan." He laughed self-consciously, and then changed the subject. "How's Brice doing?"

"Oh, he's great." Her expression softened at the mention of her son. "And growing like a weed. He's packed on another two pounds since our last visit to the pediatrician."

"And it looks like you've lost that and then some." His gaze meandered down and when interest sparked he told himself it was a natural reaction that had nothing to do with Morgan personally.

"I've been trying," she admitted. "I have an entire wardrobe I'm eager to fit back into. You may not believe this, but I do own more than baggy shirts." She tugged at the hem of the one she was wearing.

"You look good even in that."

Her cheeks turned pink. "Can I get you a drink or something?"

"I wouldn't mind a Scotch and soda." When her brow wrinkled, he said, "I'll get it myself."

He walked to the wet bar tucked to one side

of the room. Though he wasn't much of a drinker, he kept it fully stocked. After filling a glass with ice and soda, he added a shot of Scotch. When he turned, she was seated on the sofa, feet tucked up beneath her, some papers spread out in front of her. Sheet music.

"What are you doing?" he asked, coming around the side of the couch.

"Trying to come up with song selections for a couple of my more advanced students."

That had him puzzled. "You're working?"

She glanced up. "At the south-side community center I told you about."

"But I thought you agreed not to take the job?"

"No. I agreed not to leave your apartment until your parents arrive home from Europe."

"But what about the baby?" he asked.

"Brice comes with me. It's only a few hours in the afternoon." She smiled. "He tends to sleep through most of it, even my beginner students. But when he doesn't there's no shortage of people eager to hold him. The kids adore him and so does the staff."

Her explanation baffled him even more. "I don't understand why you're doing this. You shouldn't be working right now, Morgan."

"I need to. My bank account isn't as flush as yours, which is why I'm still sending out résumés looking for a full-time teaching position."

"But you just had a baby."

"Even women whose jobs afford them a paid maternity leave would be back to work by now," she pointed out. As the soon-to-be head of a Fortune 500 company, he knew this, of course. "If I were still at a school, of course, I would have the rest of the summer off. But working at the community center isn't so bad. Actually, I find it quite satisfying, even if the instruments could all use an overhaul."

"No baby grands?"

"Nope. Not a one. The grant money the center receives only goes so far. I moved my upright piano from storage to the center just so I would have something decent to play."

"Why go to the trouble?"

"The kids." Her eyes lit up. "I've never had such interested students. Some of them come from really disadvantaged backgrounds and dysfunctional homes and yet they are every bit as enthusiastic about music as I am. That makes them a joy to teach."

"You really mean that."

She frowned. "Of course, I do." The baby began to cry then. She rose with a sigh. "Excuse me."

While Bryan waited for her to return, he sipped his drink and paced around the penthouse, noting the new touches she'd added. A floral arrangement sat on a richly patterned runner in the center of his dining-room table. He'd never eaten dinner in that room, he realized. When he ate in the penthouse, he'd either sat on a stool at the kitchen island or taken his meal into the living room to watch television. He missed family meals, the kind where everyone gathered around the table and actually communicated. He hadn't had that with his wife. After Caden was born, Bryan had thought maybe things would change. Of course, they *had* changed, just not how he'd expected or hoped.

Back in the living room he noticed a trio of fat scented candles on the fireplace mantel. They weren't just for show. Their wicks had been burned. He imagined how the room would look, awash in only their light. Cozy. Intimate. Romantic.

He took another sip of his beverage and moved on. A framed picture on one of the side tables caught his eye. In it Morgan was flanked by an older couple. She was wearing a black robe and mortarboard, clutching a diploma and grinning madly. He picked it up to study it. She looked ready to conquer the world.

"That was taken at my college graduation."

He turned to find her standing behind him. He hadn't heard her return. Instead of feeling awkward about snooping—could one snoop in his own home?—he was curious.

"Are these your parents?"

"Yes." She took the photograph from his hands, swallowing hard as she stroked their faces with the pads of her thumbs. In contrast to the radiant woman in the picture, the one standing in front of him was sad. "They were so proud of me."

"You mentioned that they were gone."

"Yes, both of them."

"Sorry," he said as she put the photo back in its place. Then he motioned with his hands. "You've added a few things to the room since you've been here, I see."

"I hope you don't mind."

"No. I like what you've done. It looks nice." In fact, it looked inviting, which was why even though he should be going, he found himself in no hurry to leave.

"Why haven't you?" At his baffled expression, she added, "Made this space more personal."

He shrugged. "I don't know. I guess I just don't see the need."

"But you've lived here for three years. Ever since your divorce." At his raised eyebrows she said, "Britney told me that."

He walked over to the couch and took a seat. He'd have to have a talk with his secretary. "What else did Britney say?"

"Not nearly enough to satisfy my curiosity," she admitted baldly. "Why don't you tell me the rest?"

"There's really not much to tell. I was married for a few years, but in the end it didn't work out, so we went our separate ways." He shrugged, even though it was hardly that simple.

Morgan settled onto the cushion next to his. "Is she one of those reasons you spoke of before? For being the way you are today?"

He sipped his drink before answering. "Yes." A single word, yet he felt as if he had just bared his soul.

"She hurt you," Morgan said. It wasn't a question, but a statement. "I'm sorry."

Bryan wasn't comfortable with her sympathy, especially because, when one got right down to it, his brother had done quite a number on her as well.

"I've gotten over it."

"Have you?"

Where a moment ago he'd been in no hurry to leave, now he stood. "I should be going. You…you're probably tired."

"Too close for comfort?" she asked. "You only need say as much. You don't need to run off."

"I'm not running." He forced himself to sit again. Then, feeling ridiculous, admitted, "Okay, I'm not comfortable talking about it. It wasn't a pleasant experience."

"I don't imagine the end of a marriage ever is, regardless of the circumstances involved. Are you sure you don't want to talk about it? I've been told I'm a good listener."

God help him, he almost did. He'd kept it bottled up inside for so long. But he shook his head, unnerved by this sudden desire to share. "No. Thanks."

"Okay, but the offer stands."

Out of the blue, he heard himself ask, "Did you love him?"

She glanced away, her cheeks turning pink even before she admitted, "I only knew him for a week."

Seven days and as many nights. Bryan's stomach clenched.

"Some people fall in love at first sight, or so they claim."

Her gaze reeled back to his. "Is that what you want to hear?" she asked. "That I saw Dillon across a crowded room and—*bam!*—lost my heart to him?"

"Yes. No!" His hands were fisted at his sides. He loosened them, shrugged. "It doesn't matter. Your relationship with Dill is no more my business than the relationship I had with him is yours."

That was the end of it, he thought.

Discussion over. But Morgan said quietly, "Just for the record, I'm not…promiscuous."

Her face flamed red, giving her words even greater credence. Guilt nipped at Bryan as his thoughts turned to the probe he'd initiated into her background a few weeks back. Call it off, his gut told him. Get the facts, his head insisted. It wasn't like him to be so damned indecisive.

He shoved a hand through his hair. "Dill could be irresistible," he allowed.

"Yes, well, I'm usually pretty good at resisting, but I was at a low point in my life. A really low point. It's not an excuse for my behavior," she said quickly. "But it is a fact."

"Do you regret it?"

"How can I? I have Brice," she reminded him. "If I regret my actions, I'd have to regret him. And I don't. He's the best thing that's ever happened to me."

He swallowed, nodded. "I'll go now."

"Your clothes."

"I'll get them another time." As he started toward the door, he admitted, "I shouldn't have come in the first place."

"Why did you, then?" Morgan asked.

In the foyer, she retrieved his coat from the closet and handed it to him. Their fingers brushed, the contact fleeting. It sent shock waves through him just the same. Need built, both dangerous and exciting. Why had he come? Suddenly, he knew.

"I shouldn't have," he said again.

But she was just as persistent. "Why?"

"You don't want to know, Morgan."

"Yes, I do."

"Because of this."

He dropped the coat to the floor and cupped her face in his hands, drawing her to him even as he leaned down. His mouth was impatient, greedy. Hers was pliant, giving. So much so that even though the kiss began as an almost furious assault, it was an apology, an entreaty by the time it ended.

They stared at one another, their labored breaths seeming to echo off the marble floor. And because all he wanted to do was reach for her again, he scooped up his jacket, yanked open the door and left.

Morgan couldn't believe he'd kissed her. For that matter, she couldn't believe the way she'd responded. How could she expect him to accept her claim that she wasn't promiscuous when she'd welcomed—indeed, reveled in—every second of their intimate contact?

But while she stood in the empty foyer and waited for shame to wash over her, it never came. And when she lay in bed later that night, still too keyed up to sleep, the only regrets she felt were that Bryan still didn't completely trust her and that she hadn't experienced this kind of white-hot attraction for her baby's father.

CHAPTER FIVE

THE following week passed without a word from Bryan, and then a second one did, too. She wasn't sure whether to be grateful or disappointed. She still grew warm every time she recalled that kiss, and, God knew, she thought of it often enough.

Did he?

She managed to push that question to the recesses of her mind only to have it spring front and center again when he called her on Friday evening.

"Morgan, it's Bryan," he said unnecessarily. It wasn't as if she had many callers, let alone a male one with such a deep and sexy voice. "Are you free tonight?"

The question startled her, so it took her a moment to answer. In fact, she didn't answer. She asked a question of her own. "Why?"

"There's something we need to discuss."

That sounded ominous and made her only a little more nervous than the thought that he might be asking her out. Maybe her reaction to his kiss had finally prompted Bryan to seek a paternity test.

"Have you eaten yet?"

She glanced at her watch. It was nearly seven o'clock. "Two hours ago. If a bowl of cereal can be considered dinner."

There was a slight pause. Then he said, "I could pick up Chinese food on my way over. There's a great place just around the corner from the penthouse. Interested?"

Though she wasn't quite sure what to make

of his offer, she said, "I like chicken and peapods, skip the egg roll and fortune cookie, and make sure to get white rice instead of fried."

She thought she heard him chuckle. "I'll see you in half an hour."

Unfortunately, he was as good as his word, arriving on her doorstep just as she finished feeding Brice, who'd sent up a squeal almost as soon as she'd hung up the phone. That meant she hadn't had a chance to do anything with her appearance. She was still wearing the loose-fitting tank-style dress she'd put on to go to the center. Her hair was pulled back in a clip at her nape, although several curls had made their escape and whatever makeup she'd put on that morning was long gone.

The baby was in her arms when Morgan opened the penthouse door. Bryan's gaze drifted to the infant, the tight line of his mouth softening. Was it because he saw his brother there? More and more, Morgan thought she caught glimpses of Dillon or some trait that surely was more Caliborn than Stevens.

Or was Bryan recalling that the last time the two of them had stood in the foyer, they'd kissed? His gaze was on her now—specifically, on her mouth. She waited, certain he was going to bring it up. But he didn't and she didn't know whether to be relieved or disappointed. Did that mean she was the only one who'd spent time obsessing over that earth-shattering lip-lock?

He ended the potent silence by holding up a brown paper bag. "Shall we eat in the kitchen?"

She nodded. "No sense breaking out the fine china for takeout."

Morgan retrieved Brice's bouncy seat from the bedroom and joined Bryan as he set the granite-topped island with two plates and cutlery.

Glancing up, he asked, "Can I get you something to drink?"

"That's all right. I'll get it." She set Brice in the seat and poured herself a glass of milk. "Do you want some or would you prefer—what was it?—Scotch and soda?"

"I'll just have water tonight."

She waited till they were seated to say, "So, what did you need to discuss?"

"A couple of things, actually." He selected one of the cartons and forked out some white rice. "First, Windy City Industries would like to make a donation to the community center."

She blinked in surprise. "That's very generous. They'll be thrilled with any amount, I'm sure."

"Not money. Well, not directly anyway. Your supervisor will be notified, but basically you'll need to make up a list of the instruments you require for the after-school program you teach. We'll see to it that whatever is on the list is purchased and gets delivered as soon as possible."

"Bryan, I don't know what to say. Other than thank you, of course." She beamed at him. "You have no idea what a tremendous gift you're giving these children."

He brushed her gratitude aside. "It's not me, Morgan. The donation is coming from Windy City Industries. We believe in being community-minded and supporting worthwhile causes. I thought an after-school music program for at-risk kids was just such a cause and passed the recommendation to the appropriate people at the company to make the final judgment. They notified me today of the gift."

"Well, pass my thanks along to Windy City then." She smiled at him. He might try to distance himself from the donation, but they both knew he was responsible.

"And now to the other matter." He cleared his throat. "Unless their plans change, my parents will be returning from France the Friday after next."

"Oh." She gulped and a peapod nearly stuck in her throat. The hour of reckoning would soon be at hand.

"I'll make the appropriate arrangements once they arrive and settle in," he said.

Then Morgan's eyes widened as another thought crossed her mind. "You'll need your apartment back."

That had been the deal they'd struck when she'd agreed to stay. She'd been paying him for the privilege, not that he'd cashed the checks she'd made out to his name.

"There's no hurry," he said.

Morgan set her fork aside. She'd been

looking for a new place, and had a couple of leads on efficiencies that were in her price range. It was time to get off the fence and put down a deposit.

"When do you need me to leave?"

"Whenever," he answered vaguely.

"Don't tell me you're enjoying staying in your boyhood room?" she teased.

He merely shrugged. "Actually, my parents have a guest house at the back of their property. Dill lived there on and off. I've been using it while you've been here. It's quite comfortable, especially since there's a pool and hot tub practically outside my door."

"Well, as long as you're sure I'm not putting you out." She picked up her fork again and pushed a piece of chicken around on her plate. "Britney mentioned the commute when Brice and I first moved in here."

He frowned. "Britney talks too much."

"I probably shouldn't say this, but she's got a serious case of the hots for you."

It might have been a trick of the lighting, but she thought he blushed. Regardless, he didn't look comfortable. "Beyond the fact that I'm her boss, and not in the market for either a sexual-harassment suit or a serious relationship, she's not my type."

"She said the same thing about me." Morgan wanted to kick herself as soon as the words left her lips; instead she plowed ahead. "What is your type?"

His gaze was steady, piercing, actually. It probably scared most people witless, but Morgan didn't blink. He was good at pushing people away, but she was even better at hauling them close. She came by the talent naturally. Her father had been a pro at getting her to open up and share her feelings.

After a moment, he picked up his napkin.

Folding it into smaller squares, he said quietly, "I used to know what I wanted. Now I'm not so sure."

She knew exactly what he meant. Tall, dark and brooding had never been her ideal. Although lately…

He pulled her from her musing by saying, "About the penthouse. Don't worry about packing up for the time being. You're not putting me out. As for my parents, I'll get together with them as soon as they've recovered from jet lag, explain everything and set up a meeting."

"I'd prefer that you set up a visit," she corrected. "A meeting implies business. Business, to me anyway, implies money. I want it to be clear that's not what I'm after. I want a family for my son. Specifically, grandparents, since both of my folks are gone." She tilted her head to one side. "I also wouldn't mind an uncle, since as an only child I can't provide Brice with one of those. Do you understand?"

God help him, he was starting to. More of the old distrust melted away. Morgan was so real and pragmatic. Her feet were planted firmly on the ground. She took on the yoke of responsibility without complaint. He couldn't help wondering, he couldn't help asking, "What in the hell did you see in my brother?"

Her eyes widened. "I...I..."

"Don't answer that question!" Bryan stood so quickly he knocked over his water. The glass cracked and water sloshed across the granite before spilling over the edge and forming a puddle at his feet.

Morgan was up in an instant, grabbing a dish towel to mop up the mess on the island. When she bent down, he knelt beside her, his hand over hers on the towel. "Don't answer the question," he said again, this time more softly. "It came out wrong. For all of my brother's faults, he was a good man."

And Bryan missed him. God, how he missed him.

"I believe that, too." They both stood. "And, since I would love to hear you talk about him more and, you know, share the kinds of things I can pass along to Brice, I'm relieved you feel that way."

He waited until she returned from dumping the soaked towel and broken glass in the sink, to ask, "Why wouldn't I?"

She settled back onto her stool. "Well, the name thing for one. Some people would have been upset about that, especially since I get the feeling it wasn't a one-time occurrence."

"No, it wasn't." He sighed and sat as well. "When he was killed in Vail, the police first notified my parents that I was dead. Since I was having dinner with them at the time, we all realized what must have happened. Still, we held out hope that it was all just a big mistake and that Dill would come waltzing through the door."

"I'm so sorry."

"I flew to Vail to make a positive ID." His chest ached as he recalled the shock of seeing his brother's body on a cold metal slab at the morgue.

"My God! How horrible."

"Yeah, but better me than my mother or father. No parent should have to go through that."

"No parent should have to lose a child, period."

The ache in his chest intensified. There was more than one way to be robbed of that joy. She laid a hand on his arm. How was it possible that such a simple touch could offer so much comfort?

"You're probably wondering why Dillon did

what he did." When Morgan nodded slowly, he decided to tell her. She had a right to know. "He was pretty much broke."

If the news disappointed her, it didn't show. Her expression never wavered.

"He had a trust fund, a sizeable one, left to him by our grandparents, same as I did. I invested most of mine. He spent his. Most of it was gone by the time he got out of college."

"Didn't he work?" She did look disappointed now.

"He had a position at the company." Their father would have gladly made Dill a vice president if he'd shown any interest or initiative. "He showed up sometimes, but he didn't put in regular hours. Dill was… He never really grew up."

"And so you let him use your identity and spend your money?" Her tone held an odd mix of disbelief and censure.

"He was my brother. I looked out for him." Guilt nudged Bryan as he recalled that final phone message he'd left. Perhaps that's why his voice was hoarse when he added, "I'd been looking out for him since we were kids."

"Maybe that's why he never grew up," Morgan answered quietly. "He never had to deal with the consequences of his actions."

Anger came fast. Bryan welcomed it since it not only chased away the grief and guilt he felt over his brother, it corralled his wayward interest in this woman who was off-limits to him. She was his late brother's conquest. The mother of Dillon's child.

"I don't recall asking for your analysis," Bryan snapped, even though he knew she'd merely said aloud what he sometimes thought. That between his parents and himself they'd made it too easy for Dill.

"I'm sorry," she said. "You're right. I didn't

mean to be judgmental. We all have flaws and, as you said, despite those, Dillon was a good man." Her gaze veered to Brice. "That's what I'll make sure my son understands about his father."

"Thank you."

"You've never held him, you know."

Bryan didn't feign ignorance, rather he ignored the question, forking up a bite of sweet and sour pork instead.

"What is it about him that makes you hold back?" Morgan persisted.

God, the woman was blunt. He knew hardened dealmakers who weren't as adept at going for the jugular. Brice came to Bryan's aid. Without any fussing at all, he spat up all over his pajamas.

Morgan crinkled her nose. "Sorry about that. We're working on his table manners."

"That's all right."

She tipped her head to one side. "You're really not grossed out."

"He's a baby."

"A lot of men would be, unless they're dads themselves." Morgan used her napkin to mop up what she could before scooping the baby out of the seat. It was just as well she wasn't looking at Bryan. Her offhand comment had landed a direct hit.

After she left the kitchen, Bryan picked up his plate and dumped his uneaten dinner down the garbage disposal. His appetite was gone, obliterated by a powerful and confusing mix of emotions. He decided to leave before she started asking more questions that he didn't want to answer. Questions whose answers he was no longer sure he knew.

He was on his way to the bedroom to tell her goodbye when a knock sounded on the door. He could hear Morgan talking to Brice in the nursery. Since she was busy and this was still his penthouse, he decided to answer the door.

Courtney was on the other side, wearing a low-cut black dress and stiletto heels. Just what the doctor had ordered in the past, but seeing her crimson lips bow with promise now did nothing for him.

"The doorman said you were home. Hope you don't mind my popping by. I'm celebrating the fifth anniversary of divorce." She held out a bottle of Dom. "Want to join me? I hate drinking alone."

He glanced over his shoulder, nervous for no reason that made sense. "I'm…I was just on my way out, actually."

"Let's stay in for a little while," she coaxed, walking past him into the foyer.

"I can't stay here." He expelled a breath.

"Okay. We can go to my place," she suggested.

Take her up on the offer, he ordered himself.

Go and forget about everything for a few hours. That was what he'd done in the past. But he shook his head. "Not tonight."

"Oh? Not in the mood?" There was nothing Courtney found more exhilarating than a challenge. Her brows rose and she set the bottle of champagne and her handbag on the entry table. "Perhaps I can change your mind."

She reached for him, but before her arms wound around his shoulders Bryan trapped her hands in his. He brought them to his lips for a kiss. The gesture wasn't intended to be seductive. It was a goodbye. He could tell she knew it even before he said, "I'm sorry."

She stiffened for a moment, but then was laughing huskily. "Who is she, Bryan? Please tell me it's not that snooty little secretary that glares daggers at me every time I stop by your office."

He really had to do something about

Britney. But back to the matter at hand. "She's no one you know."

Courtney pulled away and turned, regarding him in the foyer mirror. She sounded genuinely interested when she asked, "Is she worth it?"

He glanced toward the bedroom. "It's not like that."

Courtney, of course, didn't see it that way. Turning, she said, "It's exactly like that, Bryan, or you'd still be interested in what I have to offer."

"You do have a lot to offer," he replied in lieu of an answer to her initial question.

Taking Courtney's bejeweled hands in his, he raised them to his lips again. This time the kiss he dropped on her knuckles held an apology.

Morgan, however, was the one who said the words aloud. "I'm sorry."

Both he and Courtney turned. Morgan was holding a freshly changed Brice, her eyes wide and assessing, her expression disappointed. In him?

"Oh, my," Courtney told Bryan. "Now I can see why you said 'not here.'"

"Courtney Banks, this is Morgan Stevens. She's my…she's my late brother's…." He motioned with his hand, not sure what word to use to fill in that last blank.

The baby in Morgan's arms apparently clarified things for Courtney. "Ah. I see."

"I didn't mean to interrupt," Morgan said. She would no longer meet Bryan's eye. "I just wanted to tell you that I'm going to put Brice down."

"I was just going anyway," Bryan said. Why did he feel like such a heel? He had nothing to hide. He'd done nothing wrong. The kiss he and Morgan had shared came to mind. *Liar.*

"Well, thanks for the takeout. It was nice to meet you, Courtney."

"The same here." Courtney gathered up the champagne and her handbag.

He wasn't leaving with her, but Bryan knew that was exactly what it looked like. Maybe that was for the best. "I'll call you when I hear from my parents," he told Morgan.

Her forced smile was the last thing he saw before closing the penthouse door.

"I'll see you to your car," Bryan said to Courtney as they stepped into the elevator.

She was quiet during the ride to the lobby. He appreciated her silence. He didn't want to answer questions right now. He walked her to her car, a sleek red foreign number that was parked in the fire lane.

"You're lucky you haven't been ticketed or towed," he remarked.

"I like to live dangerously," she said with a delicate shrug of her shoulders. Then, more seriously, she added, "Take care, Bryan. Don't let her hurt you."

"She's…we're not in the kind of relationship that allows for one to be hurt."

"But you'd like to be."

He opened the car door for her and ignored the comment. "I can't be hurt, Courtney."

"Sure you can. We both can be. By the right person. And we were in the past, which is why we've sought out one another's company these past few years. It's been safe."

"It's been more than *safe*," he pointed out in an effort to soften their goodbye.

Courtney's laughter was bawdy as she slipped into the driver's seat. "Well, that goes without saying. We've had some good times. I may even miss you." She pointed back toward his building. "If things don't pan out the way you're hoping, be sure to call me.

The Dom will be gone by then, but I'll spring for a new bottle."

He smiled, but made her no promises. After his divorce he'd stopped making promises to women. Or maybe he just hadn't met a woman who'd changed his mind. Until now.

CHAPTER SIX

MORGAN grew anxious waiting for Bryan to call. Not, she assured herself, because she felt he owed her an explanation as to how he could kiss her so passionately and fail to mention he had a girlfriend—a gorgeous, perfectly coiffed, perfectly proportioned girlfriend who looked as though she'd just stepped out of the pages of a fashion magazine. No, she wanted to know if he'd spoken to his parents and how they had taken the news about Brice.

Already she'd been apprehensive about meeting the Caliborns. She was doubly so now. She'd conceived a child with one of their sons during a brief fling in Aruba, and now, just months after giving birth, she found herself disturbingly attracted to the other one.

What would they see when they looked at her? A conniving gold digger? An opportunist? Someone of low moral character?

What would they see when they looked at her son? Would they too question Brice's paternity, perhaps even demand a test? It still surprised her that Bryan hadn't done so yet, because even though his attitude seemed to have softened, he remained detached from the baby.

By the time the following Friday rolled around, she was a bundle of nerves, though it helped to be busy at the community center, so she'd stayed late to help a young girl practice scales. Carla was ten and had just signed up for the program the week before. She was shy and introverted, but, like the other kids, eager to learn.

The girl's fingers stumbled over the keys of Morgan's old upright. Carla missed a couple of notes, went back to find them and winced when the wrong ones came out.

"Sorry."

"Don't apologize. Just do it again. Practice is the only difference between you and me. I've had years of it."

"You think I can be as good as you someday?"

"Maybe even better if you stay with it. Remember to invite me to see you play Carnegie Hall."

"Have you played there?"

"Twice. Now play."

The girl flashed Morgan a grin and started again, this time finishing with only a couple of minor mistakes. In his car seat on the floor next to the piano, Brice let out a delighted squeal when Carla was done.

"See, even the baby thinks you've improved."

"Thanks, Ms. Stevens. I appreciate the extra help."

"Don't mention it. It's been my pleasure. Is someone coming to pick you up?"

"My mom. She told me to wait for her at the front door so she doesn't have to find a parking space."

"Okay. Have a good weekend."

Morgan stood and gathered up some sheet music from a nearby stand. When she turned, Bryan was leaning against the jamb of the door through which Carla had exited. His suit coat was slung over one shoulder and he was watching her with dark, unreadable eyes that left her feeling far too exposed.

"How long have you been standing there?"

"Long enough. Carnegie Hall twice, hmm? You must be very good."

She lifted her shoulders in lieu of an answer. "Are you here for a lesson?"

"That depends."

"On what?" she asked.

"On what you're offering to teach me."

His reply raised gooseflesh on her arms. Morgan cleared her throat and glanced away. "In addition to the piano I play the oboe and clarinet. I'm passable on sex—*sax*."

His brows rose at the Freudian slip, but Morgan noted thankfully that he let it go without comment. He pushed away from the doorjamb and came fully into the room. "My parents are home. I spoke to them last night. They're eager to see Brice and to meet you, too, of course."

Nothing like being tacked on as an afterthought to make one feel welcome, Morgan groused internally.

Brice cooed and Bryan's gaze shifted to the baby, who was batting his chubby fists against a string of colorful rings that Morgan had draped over the carrier's handle. Bryan's expression softened. She saw him swallow hard before glancing away. Did he see his brother in the baby? Was he missing him? Could it be that that was why he sometimes seemed so sad when he looked at Brice? Now wasn't the time to ask such questions, though. Other ones needed to be answered first.

"When do your parents want to meet me? And where?"

He laid his coat on top of the piano and sat down on the bench. "They're leaving that up to you."

That news had Morgan slumping down next to him. The bench was small. Their hips bumped. She could smell his cologne. It was the same scent he'd worn the day he'd kissed her. She was inhaling deeply, even as she tried to focus on the matter at hand.

"The sooner—"

"The better," he finished for her. His gaze was locked on her mouth. She swore he leaned closer for a moment, before he pushed to his feet and took a few steps away. "That's what my parents said, too."

"How about next Saturday?" That would give her a week to rehearse what she was going to say and to find something suitable for her and Brice to wear.

"That leaves where."

"Well, I can't very well invite them to your apartment. Of course, they probably know I'm staying there since you're living in their guesthouse."

"Yes. They think I'm chivalrous."

"I can only imagine what they think of me," she remarked dryly. She turned on the bench and played the opening chords to one of her favorite concertos. "I suppose we could have dinner at a restaurant, although that seems a little impersonal. Not to mention that we wouldn't be able to talk freely without the risk of being overheard." She sent a smile in his direction and added, "My name may not be as well known as your family's, but I'm every bit as eager as you are to keep it out of the tabloids."

"In that case, I suggest that you and Brice come to my parents' estate."

She stopped playing. "You want me to invite myself to their home? Gee, should I tell your mother what to serve for lunch, too?"

He surprised her with a chuckle. "If you'd like."

"I'm serious, Bryan."

"So am I. Outside of my penthouse, the location makes the most sense."

She sighed, because he was right. "Okay."

"I'll set it up." He tucked his hands in his trouser pockets. "Are you heading home now?"

She nodded. "You?"

"I was thinking of stopping off for dinner first. Meal preparation isn't included with my new accommodations."

She smiled. "Mine either. But I've enjoyed having someone to do the grocery shopping for me. Not to mention the laundry and the housework. I'm getting spoiled."

"Somehow, I doubt that," Bryan replied.

He meant it. A woman who would work for peanuts in a community center teaching under-privileged kids the joy of music wasn't spoiled. That conclusion didn't surprise him as much as the fact that he felt Morgan deserved to be pampered and he wanted to be the one doing it.

His gaze dropped to her lips and he recalled that kiss. He didn't like the feelings that had begun to take root. They were the kind that held the potential to grow, spread and blossom into something that terrified him. His dealings with Courtney had been blissfully straight-forward. No ties. No lies. No talk of a shared future. Which was why parting the other night had been managed so easily and so affably. There were no messy emotions to get in the way. No explanations required.

But he heard himself offer one to Morgan now.

"Courtney and I…we're not seeing one another any longer."

"Oh?" Her brows notched up. "I'm sorry."

"Do you mean that?" he asked quietly.

She glanced away. "Of course I do. She seemed…nice. And she's very pretty. You made a handsome couple."

"Did we?"

"Yes. You're both very…" She lifted her shoulders. "You turn heads."

He wasn't a vain man. Nor was he one who required his ego to be stroked. But he asked, "Turn heads?"

"You have a commanding presence."

He laughed. "Some people just call me intimidating."

"Do you try to be?"

"Sometimes," he admitted. "It has its uses."

She shook her head. "I think it gets in the way of real relationships. How long were you and Courtney together?"

Bryan thought back. "Since just after my divorce was finalized."

"So a few years. It sounds like it was serious."

"No. It wasn't like that. Actually, it was...pretty casual." He frowned.

"Well, I hope my being in your penthouse had nothing to do with your split."

"No." But it did. It had everything to do with it, Bryan realized, because suddenly *pretty casual* wasn't enough. His frown deepened. "I can't figure out what it is about you that..."

"What?"

He left his previous thought unfinished and said instead, "You don't fit into any mold."

"Then why do you keep trying to force me into one?" she asked.

"Habit."

"It's a bad one. Break it." Her gaze held a challenge.

"I don't know if that would be a good idea." He tilted his head to one side.

"Why?"

A million reasons came to mind. The one he offered rose from his subconscious. "You're dangerous, Morgan."

She blinked in surprise. "Dangerous. Me?"

Yes, he thought. From the moment he'd met her she'd been a blight on his peace of mind. He wanted it back. Even more, though, he wanted…her.

He shot to his feet. He should go. Hell, he shouldn't have come. He could have called

Morgan with the information about his parents. He could have had Britney call her, for that matter. But he'd wanted to see her and he'd figured a public place was safer than stopping in at his penthouse.

And so was a restaurant, his libido offered slyly. What could happen in a restaurant with a table between them and waiters and other patrons around?

"Would you and Brice like to have dinner with me?" he asked.

"Now?"

"Now."

"I can't. Sorry. I'm nearly out of diapers and he's going to need to nurse soon."

He nodded. "I understand." Just as well, he decided. Just as well.

"May I have a rain check?"

Bryan shrugged. "Sure."

* * *

It was hot when he arrived home an hour later. He'd been hungry when he stopped at the community center. He was starving now and it had nothing to do with the fact that he'd skipped dinner.

He bypassed the main house, even though he knew his parents would welcome a visit from him and would gladly ask their cook to whip up a meal. Instead, he headed to the guesthouse and changed into his swim trunks.

A moment later, he was diving into the deep end of the in-ground swimming pool, powerful strokes taking him to the far side in a matter of seconds. Just before reaching it, he flipped and pushed off the wall with his feet. The water was cool on his heated skin and the exertion took the edge off his frustration. When he hoisted himself out of the water twenty minutes later, his mother was holding a towel, which she handed to him.

Julia waited till he'd dried off and caught his breath before asking, "So, did you talk to her?"

"Yes. I suggested that she come here."

His mother nodded. "Good, good. Well, as long as she won't find that too intimidating."

Rough laughter scraped his throat. "I don't think *anything* intimidates that woman."

"Oh?"

He cleared his throat. "We set it up for next Saturday. I didn't pin down a time. I figured I'd ask you what worked best first."

"See if one o'clock is acceptable and tell her we would like her and the baby to come for lunch." She rubbed her hands together in an uncharacteristic show of nerves. "Do you know what she likes to eat?"

His mother's question had him chuckling since it echoed Morgan's earlier comment. "I can ask her if you'd like."

"Yes. Do that. I want everything to be

perfect. Oh, my God." She covered her mouth with her hand for a moment. "I still can't believe it."

"Mom," he began, not sure how to proceed. "There's no concrete proof that she's telling the truth."

"Yes, so you mentioned when we first came home and learned that she'd been here since the end of May." Her tone held censure and more than a little hurt. Julia hadn't been happy that he'd kept Morgan and Brice a secret. His father wasn't pleased either, though Hugh at least understood and accepted Bryan's reasoning.

"Why haven't you sought that proof?" she asked now.

All it would have taken was a swab from the inside of Brice's mouth and one from Bryan's. Since Dillon was dead, short of having his body exhumed, that was the only way to establish a link between the baby and the Caliborns.

"The last thing we need is for the press to get wind of our family requesting *another* paternity test," he said tightly. "The slowing economy is already giving our investors enough reasons to worry."

"Very well, but you've met her, Bryan. You've spent time with her and you've seen the baby. Tell me, do you really think she's lying about Dillon being the father of her child?"

"No. Not lying."

"But you think she could be wrong about… the circumstances," Julia allowed.

I'm not promiscuous.

Morgan's words echoed in his head. Nothing about her suggested otherwise, so why hadn't he called off the investigation? Why wasn't he just accepting she was exactly what she said she was and Brice was who she claimed him to be?

Perhaps because he was scared to death of the attraction he felt for her.

With a muttered oath, he shoved the wet hair back from his forehead. "I don't know what I think anymore, Mom."

Julia laid her hand against his cheek. It was the same hand that had soothed his hurts when he was a kid. As comforting as he still found it, he knew it wasn't going to set things right this time.

"This must be especially hard for you, Bry."

"It's dredged up a lot of memories," he admitted. "None of them very pleasant to recall. Caden turned five a few weeks ago. I still think about him, you know."

"I know."

"The happiest day of my life was the day he was born." He'd been in the delivery room, gaping like a fool as he'd watched the miracle unfold. "I was the first person to hold him when he came into this world," he whispered hoarsely.

And he'd been among the last to learn of his wife's duplicity thanks to the DNA test results that were leaked to the media.

"We loved him, too," his mother reminded him. Julia's voice was filled with the same tangle of emotions that had Bryan's throat aching and his eyes stinging. "What Camilla did to you—what she did to us all—with her lies, it was wrong. More than wrong. It was cruel. But at some point you have to let go of the past and move on. It pains me to see you so lonely."

"I'm not lonely," he protested.

This was the second time in recent weeks that he'd been labeled as such, the second time he'd been told he needed to move on. He didn't like it.

His mother patted his cheek again, smiling sadly, and even though she didn't say a word, it was clear she didn't believe him.

CHAPTER SEVEN

FOR the next week, Morgan dragged poor Brice into half the stores in Chicago looking for an appropriate outfit to wear when meeting the Caliborns. Nothing in her closet would do. Well, except for the dress that Britney had selected for Morgan to wear home from the hospital in case a picture got snapped. She was averse to it for obvious reasons.

Besides, she'd lost more weight and a few more inches from her waist. She wanted to make the most of it. She owed her improved figure to yoga and running. Not the kind of running that involved lacing up high-performance shoes and heading out into the late August heat. Rather the kind involved in being a single, working mother whose car had decided it needed a rest. The ancient compact had started stalling out regularly a couple weeks earlier.

Usually, after a couple of minutes, it was kind enough to start back up, so she'd put off taking it in. Today, the engine had whined copiously and refused to switch on again. Now it was at a garage being worked on by a mechanic named Vic, whom Morgan hoped wasn't going to try to pad out the price of repairs just because she was female.

She shoved that thought from her mind. She had more important things to worry about, such as what she was going to wear to meet the parents of the now-dead man who had fathered her child. Outfitting Brice had been easy and affordable. As a shower gift one of the other teachers had given her an adorable sailor suit. It was in a bigger size, but he'd grown enough to wear it. Finding something for herself was proving far more frustrating.

All she knew from her brief conversation with Bryan earlier in the week was that his parents were expecting her and Brice at one o'clock on Saturday at their Lake Forest home. Lunch would be served in the garden, weather permitting. Somehow she doubted they were going to gather around a picnic table and eat franks and beans. More likely, the Caliborns would serve fancy little finger sandwiches stuffed with things like cucumbers, alfalfa sprouts and watercress.

"I don't think I like watercress," she muttered as she rummaged through the clearance racks in Danbury's.

It was the third department store she'd been to this day and it would be the last since she had to work later that afternoon. Without her car, she and Brice would be taking the El before transferring to a bus and then hoofing it three blocks to the community center.

From the final rack, Morgan pulled out a yellow sundress. Holding the hanger just below her chin, she asked Brice, "What do you think? The price is right at half off."

He yawned up at her from the stroller before smacking his lips together, clearly unimpressed.

"You're right. The color will make my skin look sallow."

Sighing, she put it back. Another two hours wasted. Or maybe not, she thought, spying the moss-colored suit on a mannequin in the department across the aisle. The jacket was short and fitted with three-quarter-length sleeves and double rows of mother of pearl buttons. The skirt flowed slightly away from the body for a fit that was sure to flatter her post-pregnancy curves without drawing too much attention to the ones she was still working to erase. She steered Brice over to it and then held her breath as she reached for the price tag.

"Oh, my God!" She swallowed. She almost prayed she was right when she said, "They probably don't have my size anyway."

They did.

"It probably won't look good on me," she said.

"Can I put that in a fitting room?"

Morgan turned to find a saleswoman standing behind her. "I—I—" With a sheepish smile, she nodded.

Not only did it fit, it looked fabulous, if she did say so herself. Even Brice gurgled happily as she modeled it in front of the changing room's trifold mirror. Of course, his exuberance may have been the result of gas since he belched loudly afterward.

"How are you doing in there?" the saleswoman asked from outside the door.

"Great. It fits and I love it. But I have one problem." Other than the price tag. Morgan stared at her reflection. "I need shoes."

She wound up walking out of the store with more than the outfit and a pair of pricy peep-toe heels. She also purchased a new handbag and had made an appointment in the store's salon for the following day. She wasn't even going to think about how much she'd just put on the charge card she kept for emergency purposes.

But late that night, as Brice slept in his crib, Morgan sat at the kitchen table sipping a cup of herbal tea and balancing her checkbook. She'd come home to a message from the mechanic working on her car. The repairs were going to total just a little less than the amount she'd plunked down in Danbury's, meaning she would have to tap the emergency credit card again.

With a sigh, she ran the numbers a second

time. In the very near future she was going to have to get a real job, a full-time position that included benefits and a pension. That made her sad. She really enjoyed sharing her love of music with the kids at the center and she felt they got something out of the experience, too.

Normally, Bryan wouldn't answer his cell phone during dinner, but when he noted the call-back number he excused himself from the table with an apologetic glance toward his mother and walked to his father's study. It was Gil Rogers, the private detective he'd hired to look into Morgan's background. He'd left a message for the man earlier in the day.

"Gil, thanks for returning my call."

"You said it was important."

"Yes. I—I decided I don't need a background check on Ms. Stevens after all. It goes without saying that I'll pay you for your services so far."

"Are you sure?" The detective chuckled then. "Never mind. I guess it makes sense. If it weren't for the baby I'd wonder if the woman wasn't a candidate for a convent. Other than a couple of boyfriends in college and an occasional date, she doesn't appear to have been involved in any serious relationships."

"So she wasn't seeing anyone else around the time the baby was conceived?"

"Not according to the people I spoke with." Gil paused. "I did learn something else, not that it has much bearing on her child's paternity, but I thought you might find it interesting."

"Go on."

"Both of her parents are dead."

"Yes, I know."

"They died together at their home in Brookside. Carbon monoxide poisoning, according to the news clips I was able to dig up. Investigators blamed it on a faulty furnace vent."

"God." The information came as a shock. He sank onto the sofa as he processed it.

"Miss Stevens found them," the detective was saying. "Her folks were still in their bed. Apparently they'd gone to sleep the night before and just never woke up. The story I read included a photograph of her collapsing in the arms of one of the fire-fighters who'd arrived on the scene. She looked pretty distraught."

Bryan closed his eyes, imagining how it must have been for Morgan and aching on her behalf.

I have no one.

She'd said that all those months ago when she'd gone into labor in his office. How horribly true her statement turned out to be.

"When did this happen?"

"A year ago last spring," Gil replied.

The information jogged Bryan's memory. More pieces of the puzzle fell into place. She would have been in Aruba just months after burying her parents. Alone, sad…vulnerable.

I was at a low point in my life. A really low point. It's not an excuse for my behavior. But it is a fact.

Bryan recalled her words that day in his penthouse. Unlike Dill, who had made excuses for everything, Morgan wasn't willing to fall back on one, even a very good one. Just as she hadn't claimed to have fallen in love with his brother, nor had she tried to gain Bryan's sympathy. Rather, she'd taken full responsibility for winding up pregnant and alone.

He thought about the check she'd written him for the use of his penthouse. Although he'd destroyed it, she'd sent him two more since then, presumably to cover each month's rent. His brother had used Bryan's name and charged his good time to Bryan's accounts. Morgan wasn't even willing to accept his hospitality.

Perhaps because she sensed his reticence.

"No more," Bryan murmured.

"Excuse me?"

"As I said, I no longer require your services," he told Gil.

"I understand, sir. But I've still got inquiries out with several people. The community where she taught in Wisconsin is pretty close-knit. It's been hard to get many people to talk. Do you want to wait until I've heard back from them?"

"No. As I said, I'll pay you for your time and trouble."

"All right." Gil's tone was reluctant. "I'll mail you a written report along with an invoice."

Bryan flipped his phone closed and tossed it on his father's desk. Then he poured himself a drink from the decanter of Scotch on the adjacent credenza. He drank it in a single gulp, closing his eyes as the liquor burned its way down his throat.

"Bryan?" His mother stood in the doorway, her concern obvious. "What is it? What's wrong?"

He was wrong.

He'd felt that way for a while now, but he had been too stubborn to admit it. He'd allowed the lies of the past to blind him to the truth of the present.

He stared at his empty glass in his hand, an idea germinating. Finally, he said, "Nothing that can't be put right."

Morgan didn't expect Bryan to come into the city to collect her and Brice on Saturday, but when he called Friday evening to tell her when he'd arrive at the penthouse, she didn't argue. Her car supposedly was repaired, but she wasn't willing to press her luck on this day of all days. Besides, she was too nervous to drive.

When the doorbell pealed, her heart was

racing. Then she opened the door, saw Bryan and she swore it stopped beating. She'd always found him imposing and dangerously handsome. Today, in place of the corporate attire she associated with him, he wore tan slacks and a white oxford-cloth shirt open at the throat. He looked younger and far less formidable than he did wearing his usual pinstripes and power tie.

He smiled. She wasn't sure she'd ever really seen him do that. And the word *sexy* got tagged on to her description.

"Wow."

His brows rose in question and she realized she'd uttered the word out loud. As cover for her foolishness, she added, "You're right on time."

"I'm always on time."

"Yes." But she'd been hoping he would be late.

She stepped back to allow him in. When she

turned after closing the door, he was watching her. Indeed, he was looking at her as if he'd never seen her before.

"The outfit is new," she said, in case that was the cause for his bafflement. "I felt the occasion called for it. Does it look okay?" Before he could respond, she added, "And just let me say, given what I spent on it, your answer had better be yes."

He didn't smile at her joke. Instead, he said most seriously, "Turn around, Morgan."

Feeling a little ridiculous, she nonetheless managed a slow twirl. "Well?"

"You've done something different with your hair." He made a vague motion with his hand.

"I had it cut. I was due for a new style." The result was a sleeker look that framed her face before flipping up slightly at her shoulders.

"It looks…you look… You're beautiful, Morgan. Stunning, in fact."

He said it the way he said everything: definitively and in a tone that allowed no argument. Not that he was going to get one from her. If the man wanted to call her stunning, who was she to quibble? Unlike Dillon's profuse flattery, Bryan's statement was all the more touching for its rareness. Something stirred in his dark eyes and for a moment she thought— and God help her, hoped—he was going to kiss her again. But then hc took a step backward and glanced away.

"We should be going."

The Caliborns' home in Lake Forest boasted more square footage than the elementary school where Morgan had taught in Wisconsin. Given its columned portico and lush landscaping, *grand* was an apt description for it. At the moment, so was *imposing*.

Bryan came around and opened her car

door. The gesture wasn't only gentlemanly but practical since she'd made no move to get out. She wasn't a coward, but she briefly considered feigning illness and asking him to take her back to the city. He seemed to understand because he offered his hand to help her out and then gave hers a squeeze of encouragement before releasing it.

"They're good people," he said quietly. "Good people who have suffered some unbearable losses."

Losses. Plural. Before she could ask what he meant, a slender woman of about sixty, wearing work gloves and carrying a trowel, came around the side of the house. She let out a squeal of excitement when she spied them and hurried forward. This was certainly a warm welcome from the gardener, Morgan thought.

"Mom." Bryan's face softened and he leaned down to kiss her when she reached them.

Mom? Morgan had been expecting a Chanel-wearing, diamond-sprinkled matriarch, not this warm and vibrant woman whose lovely face was finely etched from a lifetime of smiles that she apparently had no interest in erasing with Botox. Her hair was solid silver, not white or gray. She wore it short, in a style that flattered her oval face. Eyes every bit as dark as Bryan's dominated that face.

"Here are Morgan and Brice," Bryan was saying. "Morgan, Dillon's and my mother, Julia Caliborn."

"Hello, Mrs. Caliborn." Morgan shifted the baby to the crook of her other arm so she could extend her right hand.

"Call me Julia, please." She extended the trowel before drawing it back with a flustered laugh. "Oh, my. I'm afraid I'm not making a very good first impression. Forgive my appearance," she said to Morgan. To Bryan, she accused, "You're early."

He shook his head, looking mildly amused and all the more attractive for the smile lighting up his eyes. "We're exactly on time, Mom. You just got caught up in your garden again."

"Guilty as charged." She sent Morgan a smile. "I find playing in the dirt a good way to relax. I've been out pulling weeds and pruning plants since breakfast. Being abroad, I missed almost the entire growing season this year. I had someone looking after things here, but my flower beds are in a shambles."

"Unlikely," Bryan said. To Morgan, he added, "My mother is being modest. She's a master gardener and the estate's grounds have been featured in a couple of national publications." His pride was obvious.

Julia waved away his compliments and smiled at Morgan. Then her gaze lowered to the sleeping baby. Her voice was barely above a whisper when she said, "I'd ask to hold him, but I'm a mess at the moment."

She wasn't only referring to her stained clothes, Morgan realized, when Julia's eyes began to fill with tears. One spilled down her cheek and she swiped one away, leaving a smudge of dirt in its place. Morgan's own eyes grew moist. She'd expected this encounter to be emotionally charged for her, but she'd failed to realize how much more so it would be for the Caliborns, given Dillon's death.

"Let's go inside, Mom. Dad can keep us company while you…clean up." He handed her his handkerchief before putting an arm around her shoulders and hugging her to his side as they walked to the front door.

"Your father is probably in his study. Go visit with him while I freshen up. I won't be long."

After Julia excused herself and disappeared up the staircase that curved off from the foyer, Bryan led Morgan through the house, past the living room and formal dining room. Both rooms were every bit as lovely as she'd imagined they would be. They were filled with fine furnishings and stunning artwork, most likely pricy originals rather than reproductions. The rooms didn't appear to be showplaces, but actual living spaces. They exuded comfort and warmth and, Morgan suspected, reflected the home owners' personalities. Very different from Bryan's sterile penthouse.

More of her uneasiness melted away, but it was back in an instant when they entered the study. A man stood at the window with his back to them. He was every bit as tall as Bryan, though not quite as broad through the shoulders. Still, he was physically fit for a man in his sixties. His hair was steel gray and, when he turned, his eyes were the same tawny color Dillon's had been.

"Dad, this is Morgan Stevens. Morgan, my father, Hugh Caliborn."

"It's nice to meet you, sir."

"Morgan." The older man nodded as he stepped forward awkwardly as if not certain whether he should shake her hand or kiss her cheek. Ultimately, he did neither. To Bryan, he said, "Does your mother know you're here?"

"Yes. She came around the side of the house just after we pulled up. She'd been gardening." The two men exchanged knowing looks. "She's upstairs now changing her clothes."

Hugh nodded. Then his gaze dropped to the infant in Morgan's arms. "Bryan tells us that you named the baby Brice Dillon."

"Yes." She held her breath, waited for what, exactly, she wasn't sure.

"It's a nice name." He swallowed.

"I thought so, too."

One side of the older man's mouth crooked up. "He's just a little thing, isn't he?"

"Not so small that he hasn't already managed to take my heart hostage," Morgan mused. She still felt awed by the unprecedented wave of love she'd experienced the first time she'd held him…and every time after that.

"You'll never get it back, you know." Hugh's smile was tinged with the sadness of a father who has outlived a child.

"No," Bryan agreed. The source of his sadness had her puzzled. He cleared his throat then and suggested, "Why don't we all sit down?"

In addition to an expansive desk built of the same wood as the cherry-paneled walls, the room offered seating clustered around a fireplace. Bryan selected one of the oversize armchairs; his father took its twin, leaving

Morgan to the sofa. For the next fifteen minutes they talked about inconsequential things such as the weather until Julia, fresh from a shower, joined them.

"Hugh, goodness' sakes, haven't you offered our guest anything to drink?" she chided.

Morgan shook her head. "Oh, no thanks. I'm fine."

"I wouldn't mind a glass of iced tea," Bryan said.

"A fresh pitcher is in the refrigerator. Why don't you bring enough glasses for the rest of us just in case Morgan changes her mind."

Morgan blinked and it took an effort not to allow her mouth to fall open when Bryan rose to do his mother's bidding. Her shock must have been apparent, because after he was gone Julia turned to Morgan and said, "Everything all right, dear?"

"I didn't think anyone told Bryan what to

do." She felt her face heat and she cleared her throat. "I mean, it's just that he's so adept at giving orders, I never thought—"

God, she was digging herself a hole. But Bryan's mother was smiling as she sent Hugh a knowing look.

"Bry is much better at giving orders than taking them, which is why I try to give them on a regular basis. Someone has to keep him from becoming too dictatorial." She plucked at the buttons on her blouse as her tone turned nostalgic. "He's always been like that. Not Dillon, though. Instead of making demands, he charmed people to get what he wanted."

Didn't Morgan know it.

"Bryan and Dillon were such different personalities," Hugh agreed. "Sometimes Julia and I wondered if they'd made a pact to be polar opposites just to drive us insane." He chuckled. "Despite their differences, they were thick as thieves. There wasn't anything they wouldn't do for one another."

"It's still so hard to believe Dill's gone." Julia fell silent.

They all fell silent, except for Brice. Before the mood could become too maudlin, he began babbling happily and pumping his fists.

"Looks like you might have a prizefighter on your hands," Hugh said with a chuckle.

"He's an active baby."

"Can I… Would you mind if I held him?" Julia asked.

"Not at all."

Bryan returned to the room just as Morgan was placing Brice in his mother's arms. Morgan wondered what he was thinking as he watched Julia press her cheek to the baby's and close her eyes with a sigh. A moment later, his father was leaving his chair to perch on the arm of the sofa.

"God, it's like looking at Dill all over again, isn't it, Jule?" Hugh's voice was rough with emotion.

"Right down to the little swirling cowlick on his crown." She traced it with a fingertip.

They believed her. Their voices held no doubt, only awe and excitement. Morgan's relief was immense. She'd worried about coming here today and encountering skepticism or at the very least a cool reception. They'd welcomed her and Brice. And now they were accepting them.

From the doorway, the cook announced, "Lunch will be ready in fifteen minutes. Will you still be eating outside?"

"Yes. Thank you, Mae," Julia said. "Bryan, bring the tray of iced tea. It's too nice outside to stay cooped up in here."

She and Hugh set off with the baby, leaving Morgan and Bryan to follow. On the patio, a scrolled wrought-iron table was already set for lunch with fine china and cloth napkins. Shrubs and plants, many of them past their flowering stage, bounded the sides of the patio and spilled out into the yard. Flagstone paths led from one lush oasis to the next, as well as to a large in-ground pool. Morgan guessed the building beyond it to be the guesthouse where Bryan was staying.

"Your home is beautiful, but this—" She motioned with her arms. "This is breathtaking."

"Thank you," Julia said. "Too bad you missed it when my plants were at their peak." She shot an accusing look in Bryan's direction.

"There's next year," he said quietly.

"Yes. Next year." Julia nodded. "Do you garden, Morgan?"

"No. I lived in an apartment back in Wisconsin. I tried growing geraniums in a pot on my balcony one summer, but they only lasted until the end of June."

"I killed my share of plants, too, before I got the hang of it," Julia commiserated. She shifted Brice from one arm to the other.

"I can take the baby if you'd like," Morgan offered. "He's small yet, but he gets heavy after a while."

"Oh, no. I'm delighted to hold him." Julia laughed then. "In fact, you might have to pry him out of my arms when you and Bryan leave. You know, if you ever need a night out with friends or a little time to pamper yourself, I'll be happy to watch him for you."

"That's a generous offer."

"There's nothing generous about it. I want to spoil him rotten, as is a grandmother's prerogative." She leaned down to nuzzle Brice's cheek. The baby gurgled in response.

The sweetness of the moment had a sigh catching in Morgan's throat. This is how it would be if her own mother were alive. For the first time since coming to Chicago, she not only felt that she'd made the right choice, but that everything was going to work out. She glanced at Bryan, wondering what he thought of his mother's remark. The pain she saw in his dark eyes came as a surprise.

"Bryan tells us you've been living in his penthouse since the baby was born," Hugh said.

"Yes. I told Bryan it wasn't necessary for him to move out." She colored after saying it, realizing his parents could interpret the statement a couple of ways. "I mean, it's been kind of him to let me stay there, but I could have found another place to live. And I will, of course, now that you're home."

"What does that have to do with anything?" Julia asked. "We've enjoyed seeing so much of Bryan. It's hardly been an imposition for him to stay in the guesthouse."

"I'm relieved to hear you say that, but I think

it probably has been an imposition for Bryan, what with the commute and all." Morgan sent him a wry look.

"She's right."

"Bryan!" Julia admonished.

He talked over his mother's objection. "I would prefer to be back in the penthouse, but you needn't look at me as if I'm proposing to throw Morgan and my nephew out on the streets of Chicago to fend for themselves."

Morgan's mouth dropped open. For the first time, he'd called Brice his nephew. For a moment she thought she might have heard him wrong, but when she looked at him there was no mistaking the apology in his gaze. What had prompted his change of heart?

She was so caught up in her thoughts that she missed what else Bryan said, and so it made no sense when Julia clapped her hands together and exclaimed, "That's a great idea!

I don't know why I didn't think of it first. What do you say, Morgan?"

"Wh-what?"

"I said, I think you should move in to the guesthouse when I move back to the city," Bryan told her.

"Oh, no. No. I can't do that. You've already been so kind. All of you." She glanced around the table, her gaze lingering on Bryan. "I can't impose on your family's hospitality any longer. It's…it's not right."

"Don't be silly. We'd love to have you and Brice here," Hugh said. "For as long as you want to stay."

"And it will reduce my commute time," Bryan reminded her with a crooked smile.

Julia's argument, however, was the most poignant. "Besides, it's not an imposition. You and Brice are family."

Morgan's mouth fell open as the word

embraced her with all the comfort of a hug. She'd felt so alone, she'd *been* so alone, since losing her parents. Now here were people who had known her for less than an hour offering her not just a place to stay, but a place in their lives.

"Oh, that's…that's so…" Her eyes began to fill, and because she knew it was only a matter of time before she made an absolute fool of herself, Morgan shot to her feet.

She had no idea where she was going, only that she needed a moment of privacy to get hold of her emotions. She followed one of the flagstone paths through a rose-covered arbor, drawn by the soothing sound of rushing water. The pathway opened up to a small waterfall that emptied into a koi pond. Morgan sank down on the nearby stone bench and dropped her head in her hands, giving in to the tears that begged to be shed. When she pulled her hands away, Bryan was standing there.

"I came to see if you were all right."

As he had for his mother earlier, he offered Morgan his handkerchief.

She blotted her eyes—so much for the morning's careful application of mascara and liner—and worked up a smile. "Sorry. I just needed a minute."

"No need to apologize."

"Your mom is very kind and…" She shifted her gaze to the pond. The sight and sound of the water had a soothing effect. Bryan's presence did too. "It's incredibly lonely to be without family. I've got some aunts and uncles and a few cousins I exchange Christmas cards with. But it's not the same."

"No, I don't suppose it is."

Turning toward him, she said, "I never felt cheated to be an only child. My parents were great. Fun, funny. I could tell my mom anything, and my dad, he and I…" Her voice trailed off and it was a moment before she could continue. "When my parents were gone it was as if my whole world just stopped having any order. Suddenly, I had no place to be on Sunday afternoons. I had nowhere to go for holidays, no one to call for advice or pep talks."

"That must have been hell."

She swiped away fresh tears. "When I found out I was pregnant with Brice, my first reaction wasn't shock or desperation." She shrugged. "Oh, sure, I wasn't all that excited to become an unwed mother, especially when I found out I was about to lose my job and my health insurance. But part of me was just so relieved that I wasn't going to be alone any more."

"You're not alone, Morgan."

"I know. I have Brice."

"You have more than that." He offered his hand to help her to her feet. Afterward, he didn't let go. His fingers curled through hers.

Their palms met. "If you don't want to stay and eat lunch, I'll take you back to the city. My parents will understand."

"No. I'll stay. I finish what I start."

"I've figured that out about you."

The way Bryan was studying her made Morgan feel exposed and self-conscious. Maybe that was why she asked, "What else have you figured out about me?"

"Not nearly enough to satisfy my curiosity," he admitted. "But enough to know I owe you an apology."

"Thanks."

"Shall we?"

He was still holding her hand, the gesture friendly but somehow intimate. Though he merely led her back to the table, Morgan felt a bridge had been crossed.

On the patio, lunch was being delivered. As Mae served grilled salmon sliced over beds of crisp greens and passed out freshly baked hard-crust rolls, a younger, similarly clad woman brought a bassinet out from the house and set it between Morgan's and Julia's seats. It was white and though the wicker appeared somewhat yellowed, the bedding was obviously new.

"Thank you, Carmen." To Morgan, Julia said, "Bryan and Dill slept in this when they were infants. And Caden, too." Julia's face colored and she flashed an apologetic look in Bryan's direction.

Who was Caden?

Morgan didn't ask. Even if she'd wanted to, she didn't get the chance. She and Brice were the topics of interest in this conversation, and so, for the next forty-five minutes she answered Julia and Hugh's questions. It could have had the feel of an interrogation, but it didn't. Indeed, the Caliborns made it easy for Morgan to open up, perhaps because they'd accepted without reservation that her baby was Dillon's son.

The only time she felt awkward was when she talked about what she did for a living. Morgan didn't want her limited financial reserves to color their opinion of her.

"I'm a teacher. Unfortunately, I'm between full-time jobs right now," she admitted.

Bryan had been quiet, though whenever she'd glanced his way, he'd nodded encouragingly. Now he inserted, "Morgan teaches music. She worked in a public school district in Wisconsin, but lost her job due to budget cuts."

"That's a shame, for you as well as for the students. The arts are so underappreciated." Julia's mouth puckered in disdain. "Do you play an instrument then?"

"A few, actually, but mainly the piano."

"And she's passable at the sax." Bryan said

it with a straight face, but amusement was evident in his eyes.

God, she hoped she wasn't blushing. Clearing her throat, she said with as much dignity as she could muster, "I was classically trained. My parents had dreams of me becoming a concert pianist, especially after they'd scraped together every penny they had to send me to Juilliard."

"Juilliard?" This from Bryan, who then told his parents, "And she's played Carnegie Hall twice."

"We'd love to hear you play sometime," Julia said.

"I'm afraid I'm pretty rusty at giving concerts. These days, rather than playing Beethoven or Mozart, my time in front of the piano is largely spent helping kids learn notes and scales. I'm working a few hours each weekday afternoon in a community center." She sent a smile in Bryan's direction. "In fact,

Windy City Industries recently announced it is making a generous donation of instruments to the center."

Hugh nodded in approval. "Bryan mentioned that at dinner the other evening."

Julia looked puzzled when she added, "He neglected to tell us that you worked there."

"It's a good cause," Bryan said, shrugging.

"A very good cause," Julia agreed. "I'd imagine there are a lot of struggling families for whom private music lessons and quality instruments are beyond reach."

"Exactly. I love it, too. The kids are great, and if it helps keep them off the streets and out of trouble or harm's way, all the better."

"It doesn't pay much, though," Bryan said.

"Bryan, don't be rude," Julia chastised.

Morgan sipped her iced tea. "I'm afraid he's right, which is why I'm still sending out my résumé."

"To schools in the Chicago area?" Julia asked hopefully.

Morgan exhaled slowly. "And elsewhere. The cost of living here is a little more expensive than some of the other communities where I'm applying."

"I have a solution to that," Bryan surprised her by saying. Setting his fork aside, he reached into the back pocket of his pants and pulled out a crinkled envelope. "This is yours."

"What is this?"

"Open it."

Perplexed, Morgan did as he said, and then blinked in shock. Inside the envelope was a check. A check made out to her for the sum of two million dollars.

Bryan watched Morgan's brow wrinkle and confusion infused her expression. Glancing up, she said, "I don't understand."

"It's from Dillon's life insurance policy. He named me his beneficiary."

Shaking her head, Morgan told him, "I can't accept it," and attempted to hand back the check.

He closed his hand around hers. "Yes, you can."

"But it's yours. I don't want money." Her gaze veered to his parents then. "I didn't come here for money. Honestly, that's not…that's not…"

When Bryan squeezed her hand, she stopped talking.

"Morgan, we know that."

"Do you?" The question, dagger-sharp, was directed at him.

"Yes, I do."

Her eyes grew bright and she nodded. "But I still can't take your money."

"It's not my money. By rights, it belongs to Brice. It belongs to my brother's son."

"Bryan's right, Morgan," Julia said.

Hugh was more direct. "Dill was irresponsible when it came to his finances. Money passed through his fingers as quickly as water. Where Bryan invested the trust fund my parents left him, Dillon squandered his. In truth, I'm surprised he thought to take out a life insurance policy. He probably only did it because the father of a girl he dated in college was the principal owner of a large Chicago insurance firm." He coughed, embarrassed. "But whatever the reason, I'm glad he did it. And I agree one hundred percent with Bryan that it should go to Brice."

Morgan turned to Bryan. He was still holding her hand and could feel that she was shaking. "But Dillon named you his beneficiary. He left the money to you."

"He should have left it to Brice. I have to believe if he'd known you were pregnant, he would have. His son is entitled to that money, Morgan."

Put like that, he figured she would agree. Finally, she nodded slowly.

"Okay. For Brice."

"Good. I'll be happy to offer some advice on investments," he told her.

"Investments. Yes. I'd appreciate that." A smile loosened her lips. "I guess I don't have to worry any longer about his college fund."

"It's a wonderful idea to secure his future," Julia said. "But there's nothing wrong with also using some of it in the meantime for day-to-day living expenses, housing, trips and that sort of thing. You won't be spending it on yourself. You'll also be spending it on him."

Bryan could tell she was still struggling with the notion. Most likely because the money in question was to come from his bank account, he decided, when she asked quietly, "Are you sure you're okay with this?"

"Yes." In fact, at that moment, he'd never been more sure of anything.

CHAPTER EIGHT

MORGAN visited with the Caliborns far longer than she'd anticipated. It wasn't obligation that found her there late in the afternoon. It was their warmth and kindness. And, of course, the way they doted on Brice.

"We probably should be going," Bryan said, pushing back from the table.

"I wish this day could last forever." Julia's tone was wistful as she glanced at the baby cooing in the bassinet. "We've enjoyed this visit so much."

"I have, too. We'll get together again soon," Morgan promised.

"We'll look forward to it. It's been a pleasure getting to know you, dear. You're a very nice young woman. Exactly the sort a mother would want for her son."

Morgan smiled, but said nothing. If Dillon were still alive, would they be together now? She doubted it. Before his death, he'd made no effort to contact her. They'd made love, but they'd never spoken of a relationship. Would they have fallen in love, brought together by the shared duties of parenthood? Or, would she have come to Chicago and still wound up damningly attracted to his brother?

"Now that Bryan has given you Dillon's life insurance money, you'll probably want to invest in a home of your own," Hugh said. "But while you're looking, Julia and I still would love for you to stay in our guesthouse."

"Oh, yes. Please say you will," Julia added. "I promise not to be popping in unannounced all the time and disturbing you. Maybe just once a day to play with Brice."

Morgan had to admit, the idea of an extra set of hands held almost as much appeal as the opportunity for Brice to develop a relationship with his grandparents.

"Can that once a day be at two in the morning when he decides he doesn't want to go back to sleep?" she asked with a grin.

"Is that a yes?"

"Yes."

The older woman wrapped Morgan in a hug and rocked back and forth. "I'm so glad."

It was a moment before she stepped back. Then she said to Bryan, "Why don't you show Morgan around the guesthouse before you leave. It's in presentable condition, I hope."

"More or less."

"Good." Julia scooped up the baby. "And take your time."

"We'll be lucky to get out of here before midnight," Bryan groused good-naturedly as they crossed to the guesthouse. His tone was more serious when he added, "I'm glad you agreed to stay here for a while. It means a lot to my parents to be able to get to know Brice and have him so near. They're not very happy with me that I kept him a secret for so long."

"You did what you thought was best," Morgan allowed, though she still felt she was missing some pertinent facts. "And it means a lot to me, too, to have them so close by. Every child deserves at least one set of doting grandparents."

"They'll spoil him rotten if you're not careful. Before you know it, toys will start arriving. Big toys like motorized cars and life-size stuffed ponies." He snorted out a laugh. "They're good at that."

Morgan frowned. He sounded as if he spoke from experience, she thought as he opened the door and waited for her to go inside.

The guesthouse was much smaller than Bryan's penthouse, but what it lacked in square footage it made up for in warmth and coziness. The kitchen was outfitted with high-end appliances and warm maple cabinetry. A high counter separated it from the living room. A newspaper was laid out on the counter next to a cup of coffee and a plate dotted with toast crumbs and a small wedge of crust. She pictured him sitting there, combing through the business section as he ate.

"That looks like the breakfast of champions," she teased.

"Making toast is the extent of my culinary abilities." He shrugged. "Don't tell my mother I left dirty dishes out. She'd be appalled."

"Actually, this place is amazingly clean for a bachelor pad," Morgan remarked as he led her down a short hall.

"That's because I'm not here much to mess it up." He opened the first door they came to and switched on the light, revealing a full bath with the kind of tub a woman could do some serious soaking in and a glass-enclosed shower. Pointing to a partly opened door on the other side, he said, "You can access this room from either the hall or the bedroom."

That was their next stop. Once inside, he pulled back the drapes and light flooded in. The room was amply proportioned, although she would have to rearrange the furniture to accommodate Brice's crib and changing table. Bryan read her mind.

"If you take out the desk and move the bed over to that wall, you'll have no problem fitting in Brice's nursery."

The desk in question was piled high with file folders and a laptop computer.

"You're not home enough to mess up this place, but you find time to work here?"

"The company is in the middle of an expansion right now. Since my father is close to retiring, I'm working with the project manager to handle the details and smooth out any wrinkles that develop."

She didn't doubt he was busy, but it still sounded like an excuse to her. "You should be getting out more, spending time with people."

"Who says I don't?"

She folded her arms across her chest. "Does that mean you've found a replacement for Courtney so soon?"

"Would it bother you if I had?"

"Yes." The reply came quickly and left her blinking. It *would* bother her, she realized. A lot. In fact, just thinking about Bryan kissing another woman the way he'd kissed her that one time in his foyer made Morgan want to scream at the top of her lungs. Fortunately, her tone sounded normal when she continued. "You told me that things between the two of you were pretty casual."

"Yes. That's what I want."

Because of his divorce? It had to be. Had he been hurt that badly? "Well, I think you deserve more than that."

He looked mildly amused. "Oh, you do?"

"You're a good man, Bryan."

"Are you sure about that?"

She hadn't been when they first met, but she was now. Oh, he tried to hide it, for reasons that remained a mystery to her. But he was sensitive and fair. The instruments for the community center and the transference of Dillon's life insurance money to Brice were proof of that.

"Yes, I am. And it doesn't hurt that you're also drop-dead gor—"

She ended the description abruptly, but not before he'd figured out where she was heading with it. One side of his mouth crooked up.

"By all means, go on."

When she didn't, Bryan turned the tables on her. "What about you? You're a good person. Drop-dead—et cetera. Don't you deserve more?"

"I stopped thinking about what I deserved the moment I had Brice. I have responsibilities and obligations. I'm a mother now."

"Even mothers can get dressed up and go out on a date now and then, Morgan."

She shook her head. "Not this one."

"Why?"

The way he was watching her made it hard to think, especially since they were standing on opposite sides of an unmade bed whose tangled sheets had her mind straying into decidedly inappropriate territory. "Brice needs me."

Bryan's voice dipped low. It was a seductive whisper when he asked, "Don't you have needs?"

The question was dangerous. The answer that echoed in her head was even more so. Her gaze dropped to his mouth. What she wanted was off-limits and had to remain that way. Morgan couldn't afford to be reckless again. What if things didn't work out? Then what? She would still have to see him. Morgan might not be related to the Caliborns, but her son was. She couldn't afford to jeopardize things.

So she told him, "I have everything I need."

Bryan watched her swallow after making

that declaration. She'd sounded resolute, but the way she'd stared at his mouth told him something else.

"Same here," he said.

They were both liars.

It was growing dark when they arrived at the penthouse. Bryan found a spot in front of the building. It didn't surprise her that he came around to open her door. But it shocked her when he lifted Brice out of the car seat.

"I'll carry him," he said when she reached to take him. "That's if you don't mind."

"I don't mind." Quite the opposite. She liked seeing Brice cuddled in Bryan's capable arms as they walked to the building. "You know, I never noticed it before, but you and Brice have the same shaped eyebrows."

His tugged together. "Really?"

"Well, not when you do that."

He stopped walking. "Do what?"

"Frown." Before she could think better of it, Morgan reached up and smoothed out his brow. Afterward, she drew back her hand quickly. To cover her nerves, she quipped, "You do that a lot."

"Do I?"

"I wonder if he's going to be able to intimidate people with a mere glance when he grows up."

"It takes years of practice to perfect. I'll have to get busy teaching him."

Though his comment was offhanded, she hoped Bryan really planned to play a more active role in her son's life. That was what she'd hoped for when she'd stayed in Chicago. That was all she could hope for now.

When the elevator arrived at the top floor, Bryan remarked, "I think someone needs a change of pants."

"Give him to me. I'll take care of him."

"That's all right. I'll do it."

Morgan was aware her mouth had fallen open, but she couldn't seem to close it as she watched Bryan walk down the hall to the bedroom.

Bryan laid Brice on the changing table and rolled up his sleeves. "Try not to move around too much, okay?"

The baby kicked his legs as an answer.

"Never mind."

For the past few months, Bryan had gone out of his way not to hold the baby or touch him, even though at times he'd been tempted. Just being around Brice had brought back too many memories, and even the good ones had made him ache. He'd reached a conclusion, though. He needed to face his demons head-on and step up to the plate as the boy's uncle. This was his brother's son, Dillon's legacy, which was why Bryan wanted Brice to have the life insurance money. But money was a poor substitute for affection. Morgan and the baby needed him. A little scarier was the realization that he needed them, too.

"You'll be happy to know I'm not a novice at this."

The baby merely blinked at him.

"Hey, don't look so unimpressed."

This time Brice yawned and turned his head to one side. Bryan traced the baby's ear from the folded edge at the top down to the tiny lobe.

"It seems we have more in common than our eyebrows. The Caliborn ears. Mine are a little bigger than yours. Your dad had these, too. If you're lucky you'll inherit his ability to make people laugh. He didn't take life too seriously." Bryan shook his head. "He said I did that enough for both of us."

He swallowed then. Missing Dill. Missing

Caden. "I wanted you to be his, you know. From the very beginning I wanted you to be his. Just like I wanted Caden to be mine."

"Bryan?" Morgan stood in the doorway. "I just came to see how you were doing."

He cleared his throat. "Fine."

"I can take over if you'd like."

"No. I've changed a diaper or two in my time." He began unsnapping the blue-striped sleeper, a task made a little more difficult by the baby's flailing limbs. But he finally managed to remove it, along with the soiled diaper. A moment later he was redressing Brice, who was now cooing happily.

"I guess you *have* done that a time or two," Morgan commented.

"You doubted me?"

She nodded. "Sorry. It's just that you don't look like the sort of man who's ever pulled diaper duty."

"It has been a while."

"How long?" she asked softly.

"A few years." Rough laughter scraped his throat. "I guess that diapering a baby is like riding a bike. Once you learn how, you never forget." He lifted Brice to his shoulder. "You don't forget this, either. How they feel in your arms."

"Who is Caden?" she asked quietly.

He closed his eyes. "My…ex-wife's son."

"Oh." Morgan frowned. He could see that his reply had raised more questions than it had answered. "I thought…I guess I thought he was your son."

His laughter was harsh. "I did, too."

The story spilled out, haltingly at first as the words were wrenched from deep inside him. Through it all, Morgan said nothing, listening in that patient way of hers, her expression concerned and sympathetic rather than pitying.

"I'm sorry, Bryan," she murmured. Reaching

up, she brushed his cheeks. He'd been crying, he realized. The tears should have embarrassed him. In the past he would have considered them a show of weakness. But they were cleansing and empowering somehow. And he felt stronger.

"I wish you'd told me sooner."

Oddly, so did he. "It's not something I talk about."

"Then I'm glad you shared it with me."

Morgan put one arm around his waist and, pressing her cheek to his shoulder, hugged him. Bryan shifted Brice to his other shoulder so he could hug her back. They stood like that for a long time.

"Can I stay?" he asked quietly. "Just to sleep."

"Yes."

As Morgan sat in the rocking chair and nursed Brice, she could hear Bryan moving around in the bedroom next door. A moment later the shower switched on. The sounds were routine, domestic and oddly comforting.

After burping Brice, she laid him in his crib. He fussed before settling down, grunting as he wriggled around to find a comfortable spot.

Morgan patted his tummy and recalled what Bryan had revealed. Her heart ached for him. To have been deceived that way by someone he'd loved and trusted had left a lasting scar. No wonder he'd been so cynical and distrustful when she'd first arrived. No wonder he preferred casual relationships with women like Courtney. Would he ever be willing to risk his heart again?

Morgan kissed her fingers and touched Brice's cheek before slipping out of the room. She had no business wanting to know the answer to that question.

It was almost nine o'clock when Bryan joined her in the living room. His hair was still damp from his shower. He wore the tan pants he'd had on earlier and a white cotton T-shirt he'd culled from his dresser. His feet were bare.

She'd made a bowl of popcorn and was watching an old movie on cable. "Are you hungry?" she asked. "I can make you a sandwich or something."

He settled next to her on the couch. "That's all right. What are you watching?"

"I'm not sure. I tuned in after it started. Want some popcorn?" When he nodded, she shifted the bowl between them.

"You moved the television," he said. "And the couch."

"Yes. It made more sense over there. And, well, once I moved the television, I couldn't leave the couch where it was. I'll move it back when I leave."

"No. That's okay." He glanced around, nodded. "I like it this way. It's more… homey."

Because she didn't know what to say to that, she asked, "Speaking of moving, when are we going to make the swap?"

He rubbed his chin. "Does next weekend work for you?"

"Sure." She wiped her fingers on a napkin. "Brice and I don't have any other plans."

They finished off the popcorn while they watched the rest of the movie. As the credits rolled, Morgan glanced over at Bryan. He'd been quiet for a while and no wonder. His head was resting on the back of the couch and his eyes were closed. She reached for the remote and switched off the TV. It had been a long and emotionally draining day for both of them. If not for nerves, she wouldn't have lasted this long.

I should wake him, she thought. Let him settle into the comfort of his bed. And seek out the refuge of mine.

Morgan reached over and turned off the light. In the darkness she felt his arm come around her, stopping her from rising to her feet. She sank back on the cushion, allowed him to pull her closer to his side. Though she told herself to go, she stayed exactly where she was until Brice's cries woke her five and a half hours later.

CHAPTER NINE

MORGAN was out early Monday morning running errands when the first fat raindrops began to fall. As she hurried to her car with Brice in his stroller the front page of a newspaper caught her eye. The black-and-white photograph of her, Brice and Bryan standing on the street outside the apartment ran four columns wide. She was touching Bryan's face. Smoothing his brow that was so much like her son's, she recalled now, though the photograph made the contact appear far more intimate than that.

It didn't help that the accompanying headline read: Another Questionable Caliborn? This time Windy Cities scion in no hurry to claim child as heir.

Groaning in disbelief, she snatched a copy from the newsstand. Her dread increased tenfold as she scanned the contents of the article. Not only did it debate Brice's parentage and make insinuations about the character of the single mom who'd moved into Bryan's penthouse, it went on to rehash the horrid details of his divorce and the painful revelation that Caden was not his son. Given how violated she was feeling, Morgan could only imagine Bryan's reaction when he learned that his private life had once again been turned into a public spectacle.

She paid for the paper and tucked it into the diaper bag. She had to reach him, talk to him, offer whatever help or comfort she could. Her hair was damp by the time she reached her car. She quickly buckled Brice into his seat in the back and stowed the stroller. Then she swore under her breath when the engine refused to turn over.

"Not today!" she hollered.

Thumping the steering wheel with the palms of her hands, she debated her options. Bryan would be at the office. She needed to find a phone and call him, warn him. Unfortunately, she didn't own a cell. Yet. She would before the day was out, she decided, making a mental note. She remembered passing an El stop a few blocks from where she was parked. She was a good two miles from Bryan's office. Mind made up, she got out of the car and retrieved the stroller. Covering Brice up with an extra blanket from the diaper bag, she took off at a run.

Bryan was in a foul mood when he stepped off the elevator. He usually arrived at the office no later than seven-thirty, but he'd had a

Rotary breakfast across town, followed by a meeting with bank officials. Then he'd run into a snarl of traffic on State Street. It was almost ten o'clock now and in less than fifteen minutes he had a transatlantic conference call scheduled with the site manager and a couple of other managers concerning the London expansion project.

Britney trailed behind him into his office, going over his phone messages as he peeled off his damp coat. It was pouring outside and thunder rumbled in the distance. Everything they said about Mondays was true, he decided, and that was before he saw the tabloid on top of the stack of traditional newspapers he read each day.

At his muttered expletive, Britney said, "I'm sorry, Mr. Caliborn, but I knew you would want to see this."

No. He didn't. But he read the headline

anyway and that alone had him shouting, "Get my attorney on the phone."

The young woman nodded, but hesitated in the doorway.

"Is there something else?" He almost hated to ask.

"Yes." Her tone cooled considerably when she said, "Miss Stevens phoned you. Twice in the past hour. I'm guessing she saw the newspaper as well."

Bryan closed his eyes and sighed. To think he'd believed this ugliness was finally over and forgotten. Not only had his past been dredged up, Morgan and Brice had been dragged into it. That just plain ticked him off. Somebody's head was going to roll.

"Get her on the phone first."

"I would, but she didn't leave a call-back number."

He frowned. "She wasn't at home?"

"No. She was calling from a pay phone." Britney tugged at the hem of her jacket. "Not that it's any of my business, Mr. Caliborn, but do you think Miss Stevens could be one of the unnamed sources?"

"What?"

"In the story. It relies heavily on them."

"What on earth would Morgan have to gain by making herself the center of a scandal?" he snapped.

"I don't know. Some people enjoy notoriety and the attention. I mean, she showed up here in labor, burst in on your meeting." She coughed delicately then. "And it can pay well."

"You think Morgan sold this story to *City Talk* for money?" He wasn't angry, but incredulous.

"I hope not. For your sake, Mr. Caliborn. You've been through enough of this kind of thing. If there's anything I can do to help you, anything at all, I'll be glad to do it. But

I felt the need to raise the possibility since so much of what is printed here is, well, inside information. Who else would have known that you were so generously allowing her and her baby to live in your penthouse, even though obviously you were suspicious of her claims about the baby being yours?"

"What do you mean by that?"

"You hired a private detective to investigate her sexual history." At his raised eyebrows, she said, "I put through the invoice Gil Rogers sent with his report last week."

She also had to have read the report to know what the man had been investigating.

Bryan held up a hand. "Stop right there. I can think of a few people wise to those details, which, by the way, aren't exactly the facts. That's why I know Morgan didn't plant this story. She wouldn't have gotten things wrong.

As for needing money, Morgan is a wealthy woman in her own right these days."

"She…she is?"

"Yes. But I agree this information came from an inside source. When I find out who's responsible for this story, and I will, that person won't be working here. In fact, it would be better for that person altogether if they resigned their position and cleared out their desk before I had to ask them to do it."

Her face paled beneath her blusher. He had a sick feeling he'd just found his Judas.

"If Morgan calls back, put her through immediately."

"But the conference call…" Britney began.

He meant it when he said, "Interrupt me, if need be. She's more important."

When the conference call from London came, he still hadn't heard from Morgan. Bryan didn't like it. Where was she? Had she seen the story?

Was she being hounded by reporters? Unfortunately, he had no choice but to wait.

Bryan's mood didn't improve as he listened to the site manager rattle on about cost overruns and a couple of snags the construction crew had encountered with local officials.

Rubbing his forehead, he asked, "How much extra are we talking?"

The sum had him swearing. From the doorway, Britney cleared her throat. "Hold on a minute, John." He covered the mouthpiece with his hand. "Do you have Morgan on the line?"

"Actually, she's here."

Relief flooded through him. "Get her a cup of coffee or tea if she prefers and tell her I'll be with her in a few minutes."

It was nearly half an hour, though, before he was finally able to wrap up the call. He'd found it difficult to concentrate on the site manager's concerns with Morgan just outside his office, especially when he heard Brice start to fuss.

When he finally hung up and stepped out into the waiting area, his mouth fell open at the sight of her.

"My God! Are you okay?"

"I'm fine." She didn't look fine. Her hair was soaked and plastered to her head. Her clothes were equally soggy. Brice had fared better thanks to the stroller's hood and an extra blanket. Now that he was sipping from a small bottle of juice, he was perfectly content.

"What happened?" Bryan asked once they were alone in his office.

"I had to see you."

"Morgan, you're soaked to the bone." And cold, too, he thought as he watched her shiver. He helped her out of her wet coat and put his suit jacket around her shaking shoulders.

Together they sat on the leather couch, the same couch where she'd once writhed in labor.

"I got caught in the r-rain. My car broke d-down again."

"That thing is a hazard," he said as he rubbed her back.

"Agreed. It's gone to the scrap heap as of today. But that's not why I'm here, Bryan." She shifted so she was facing him, green eyes filled with concern. "I don't know how to tell you this, but—"

"You've seen the article in *City Talk*."

She winced. "You know."

"Britney brought in a copy." He frowned. "That's why you rushed here in the rain?"

"I tried calling from a coffee shop and again at the El stop, but this seemed the sort of thing you should be told in person anyway. I'm so sorry."

She meant that, he knew. "It's not your fault.

Hell, you and Brice are as much victims as I am. More so, when you get right down to it. You only got dragged into this because of the Caliborn name."

She tilted her head to one side. "It's a good name. One worth standing up for. Fight back, Bryan."

"Oh, I plan to. I've already spoken to my attorney about bringing a libel suit against the publisher. He thinks wc have a good case, despite my standing as a quasi-public figure. They printed half truths and outright lies without making any effort to verify the facts."

"Tell me about it. They make me out to be some sort of…" She shook her head, left the sentence unfinished.

It was his turn to apologize. He pulled her against him, dropped a kiss on her temple. "I'm sorry you got thrown under the bus with me."

"That's okay. I'm pretty resilient."

"I know." But she didn't deserve this. He stood and helped her to her feet. "Now let's get you and Brice home so you can get out of those wet clothes."

Morgan didn't expect Bryan to stay after he delivered her and the baby to the penthouse. Especially after they spotted a photographer hanging around outside and the doorman told them a couple of reporters had tried to sneak into the elevators. But he didn't leave. Instead, he offered to change and entertain the baby while she took a hot shower and put on fresh clothes.

She did so quickly, pulling her still-damp hair into a ponytail and not bothering with makeup. She didn't want to keep him waiting too long. Surely he had to get back to the office. But when she joined him in the living room, Brice was asleep in his swing and Bryan was in no hurry to leave.

He was sitting on the couch with one foot

propped on the coffee table. He'd removed his suit jacket when they arrived. His tie was loosened now, too, the sleeves of his crisp white shirt rolled halfway up his forearms.

"It's almost lunchtime. Are you hungry?" she asked.

"Not really. You?"

"No." She'd felt queasy since seeing that headline. She plunked down next to him on the couch.

"I called my parents to let them know. A neighbor saw the paper in the grocery store and had already given them the news."

Grimacing, Morgan asked, "What did they say?"

"Well, they weren't happy about it, but they were more worried about me." He sent her a smile. "And you. They're especially glad you're going to be moving into their guest-house. You and Brice will have more privacy there. They'll see to it."

"But isn't my moving there likely to raise more speculation? The last thing I want to do is cause your parents to be hounded by reporters or have photographers camped outside their front door."

He leaned forward, rested his elbows on his knees. "They have a suggestion for how we can prevent that. They want to call a press conference, Morgan." One side of his mouth rose. "Steal the gossipmongers' thunder, as my dad put it."

"A press conference?"

"They want to make it clear to everyone that Brice is a Caliborn. They don't want it to seem as if we're hiding something or are somehow ashamed of the situation." He turned, touched her face, his fingers lingering on the curve of her cheek. "But it's your decision. They're leaving it up to you."

She glanced away. "The details make it all seem so sordid."

"You don't owe them details. Just the basic facts. Brice is Dillon's son and you came here to connect with your baby's family. There's no shame in that."

"No shame in that," she repeated. Being an unwed mother wasn't as big a deal as it used to be, but that didn't mean Morgan was eager to have all of Chicago discussing her situation over their morning coffee.

"None."

She nodded as she rose and crossed to her sleeping son. Lifting him out of the swing, she dropped a kiss on his forehead. "I'm going to put him in his crib."

Bryan was still on the couch when she returned. "We don't have to say anything," he told her. "You don't owe anyone any explanations. My parents will understand."

"No." She shook her head. "I told you to stand up, fight back. I need to, too. Your parents are right. In the absence of the facts, the lies will just continue being spread."

He stood, crossed to her. Hands on her shoulders, he asked, "Are you sure?"

"Yes. I won't let my son be the subject of rumors."

Bryan pulled her close for a hug. He intended the gesture to offer reassurance, but it morphed into something else as the seconds ticked by. She fitted perfectly in his arms, soft curves molding against him. He turned his head slightly so he could breathe in her scent. It was nothing overpowering, a hint of citrus and soap. His lips brushed her temple as his hands stroked her back, and just that quickly, the need he'd tried to keep banked was stoked to life.

"Morgan." He sighed her name. "God, I

wish…" He covered her mouth with his to prevent the words from slipping out. They were too frightening, too damning to utter.

Her arms came up, her hands gripped his shoulders. He felt her fingernails dig into his flesh through the fabric of his shirt, letting him know that this need wasn't one-sided. Bryan took everything she offered and still wanted more. He'd never been this greedy or felt half this desperate. His fingers brushed her cheek, stroked the column of her neck and then found the buttons of her blouse. As he nibbled the sensitive skin just below her ear, he slipped the first one through its hole. When the last one gave way and his fingertips brushed the valley between her breasts, he was rewarded with a moan of pleasure.

"You're in—"

"Insane." Morgan finished as she pushed

away, pulling her blouse together. Her hair was mussed, half of it hanging free from the ponytail.

The breath sawed in and out of Bryan's lungs. Actually, he had been thinking intoxicating, incredible.

"I— We can't do this!"

He almost argued the point. He thought they could do it, very well and to both of their satisfaction. But he knew that wasn't what she meant.

"Can we pretend this never happened?" she asked.

They'd done that after the first time he'd kissed her. It hadn't worked for him then. It wouldn't work now. But Bryan nodded anyway. "If that's what you want."

"I think it's for the best, given everything that's involved here."

Bryan retrieved his coat. Though his body

was burning with need from their all-too-brief encounter, he said, "It never happened."

After he left, Morgan flopped down on the couch. She was mortified by her behavior. The way she'd kissed him. The thoughts that had gone through her mind at the time. Just thinking about them now had goose bumps prickling her flesh, heat curling through her…tears blurring her vision.

A year ago, confused and in mourning, she'd allowed Dillon to seduce her. She was every bit as confused now, but no seduction was necessary on Bryan's part. She wasn't sure when or how, but the fact was irrefutable. She'd fallen in love with him.

CHAPTER TEN

THE Caliborns called the press conference for the following afternoon. It made no sense to put it off, Morgan knew, especially now that the mainstream media had started sniffing around, too. But given what had transpired between her and Bryan twenty-four hours earlier, she was a nervous wreck. How was she going to stand in front of a crowd of probing reporters and explain that her relationship with Bryan was strictly platonic?

She wore the outfit she'd purchased to meet the Caliborns just the weekend before. Though she'd deposited the check Bryan had given her, she'd hardly had time to shop for something new. Vaguely, she wondered if someone would notice it was what she'd had on in the photograph that had been snapped. As for Brice, it didn't really matter what he wore. Morgan planned to have him wrapped up tightly in a blanket, allowing only minimal exposure. She wasn't about to let her son's image be exploited so they could sell more papers.

Bryan sent a car for her. The conference was slated to begin at ten o'clock at the Windy City offices. She arrived just after nine and was quickly ushered inside the same conference room where she'd first encountered the real Bryan Caliborn. He was at the end of the same long table, standing rather than sitting, and instead of a file folder, a bank of microphones was in front of him. He looked every bit as handsome and authoritative as he had that day. The only difference was that instead of scowling when he spied her, his eyes lit up and he smiled.

Julia and Hugh were there, too. Julia gave Morgan a hug and took Brice, who had fallen asleep on the car ride over. Hugh hugged her as well.

"Damned vultures," he muttered. "For all the good things Windy City Industries has done in this city, you'd think they'd show some restraint on private matters."

When Hugh released her, Bryan was there, holding out a cup of tea like a peace offering. He didn't hug her, but he did squeeze her arm when he asked, "Nervous?"

"Yes." For reasons that had more to do with the man in front of her than the throng of reporters assembling outside. "I suppose you're better at this sort of thing than I am. This is my first news conference."

"I've done several, but I'm nervous, too. I'd much rather be talking about business than about my private life," he said ruefully.

"Did you read over the notes I sent last night?"

She nodded. He had e-mailed Morgan a set of questions he felt they were likely to encounter and suggestions for how they should respond. Basically, all she had to be was honest, but brevity was the key.

"Remember, don't offer them anything they don't ask for, and feel free not to answer any question that makes you uncomfortable. They're not entitled to all of the details," he said.

She hoped it wouldn't come to that, because clamming up would defeat the purpose of such a press conference. They wanted the media to get their fill and then go away, otherwise the story would grow legs and keep running.

A knock sounded at the door a moment before a young woman poked her head inside. "The waiting room is full. Should I start sending them in, Mr. Caliborn?"

"Give us five more minutes," he said.

"Who's that?" Morgan asked.

"My new secretary." His mouth tightened.

This came as a surprise. "What happened to Britney?"

"She wisely decided it was in her best interests to resign."

They stood at the end of the room, Morgan holding Brice and flanked by the elder Caliborns. Bryan was just in front of them at the microphones. The long table kept the reporters and photographers at a distance, though close enough that Morgan saw eagerness and speculation in some of their expressions. When the noise died down and everyone had filed into the room, Bryan cleared his throat and gave his prepared statement.

"Thank you for coming here today. As you know, a story about my family recently ran in *City Talk*. It was poorly researched and full of innuendo and outright lies. My attorney will be filing a libel suit on my behalf. In the meantime, we asked you here today to set the record straight.

"First of all, the baby in question is a Caliborn."

Camera flashes popped and a couple of reporters shouted out questions. Bryan ignored them and kept talking. "His name is Brice Dillon Stevens. He is my late brother's son."

The room erupted into a frenzy then. He gave up continuing with his prepared remarks and pointed to a reporter.

"Leslie Michaelson with *City Talk*," the woman began. "I didn't write the original story that appeared in my newspaper."

"Rag, you mean," Julia inserted. The comment, coming as it did from such a demure and usually pleasant woman, had most of the reporters snickering.

The woman cleared her throat and went on, "We were led to believe, by a source very close to you, that the baby was yours. Do you deny that Miss Stevens had been contacting your office for months, seeking an audience with you regarding her pregnancy?"

"Miss Stevens did contact me looking for her baby's father. Dillon was not here, so I referred the matter to my attorney."

Morgan was impressed. What he'd said was true, he'd just left out enough information to give a different impression—much like the woman's *City Talk* colleague had done in the original story.

"My question is for Miss Stevens," another reporter chimed in. "How did you meet Dillon Caliborn?"

"I met him while vacationing. I found him very charming, and I was very sorry to learn of his death."

The man opened his mouth to follow up on the question, most likely to fill in the gaps left by her response, but Bryan called on another reporter before he could.

"Mr. and Mrs. Caliborn, is there any doubt in your mind that Miss Stevens's child is your grandchild?"

"None whatsoever." Julia beamed.

"He's a Caliborn through and through," Hugh agreed. "If he chooses, he'll be the one standing before you one day, putting you in your place instead of putting up with your nonsense."

That caused a rumble of uncomfortable laughter from their ranks.

The reporter wasn't deterred, though. This time he addressed Bryan. "In the matter of the son your former wife conceived while married to you, a paternity test was performed. Was one done this time?"

Morgan chanced a glance at Bryan. His expression was inscrutable, but she knew the pain the question caused and it was all she could do not to shout for them all to go away and leave him alone.

"No test was necessary. Unlike my former wife, I trust Miss Stevens."

"Is that why you hired an investigator to probe her background and report back on any other men she might have been seeing at the time of the baby's conception?"

Morgan hadn't seen that question coming. It landed like a prizefighter's uppercut. She let out a little gasp, which she camouflaged by clearing her throat. "I'll take this one," she said.

More flashes popped. Holding the baby so his face wasn't visible to the cameras, she stepped to the microphone.

"I requested the investigation." Morgan didn't question why she felt the need to stretch the truth, only that, even though she was hurt by the revelation, it seemed the right thing to do. "The Caliborns accepted my son and me right away. They have shown me nothing but kindness. But given what the family had been through in the past, I wanted them to be assured of my claims. Even though they saw no need for a definitive paternity test, I wanted as many facts as possible on the table."

"Are you still living in Mr. Caliborn's penthouse?" someone shouted.

"I will be moving out today and he will be moving back in. He's been very gracious to let me stay there as long as he has, and I've appreciated his kindness."

"Where will you move to?"

"Do you really think I plan to give the lot of you my new address?" she asked with wry laughter.

The reporters and photographers laughed as well.

More questions were asked, all of them antici-pated and as such easily answered. Then Bryan announced, "This will be the final question."

Morgan nearly sagged with relief until she heard what it was. Then she stiffened.

"Mr. Caliborn, what exactly is your rela-tionship to Miss Stevens?"

Had the question been directed toward her, she would be stammering over her words. But not Bryan. Without hesitation and in that tone that brooked no argument, he said, "My rela-tionship to Miss Stevens is obvious. Her son is my nephew and since my brother is no longer alive I feel an obligation to look after both of them."

His words echoed what Britney had told Morgan when she'd moved into the pent-house: *Mr. Caliborn takes his responsibilities very seriously.*

The answer was jotted down in the man's

notebook, apparently accepted as the truth, but Morgan didn't want to believe it could be possible that while Bryan was attracted to her and finally trusted her, duty was his main priority.

Bryan was grateful to see the last straggling queue of reporters file out of the conference room and pile into the elevator.

Once they were gone, Julia wilted onto one of the chairs with a sigh. "I think that went well."

"For a feeding frenzy." Hugh grunted. "But at least it's over and done with now."

Morgan was leaning against the far wall, jiggling the baby in her arms and staring intently at a spot on the carpet. She was quiet, far too quiet for Bryan's liking, and he suspected he knew the reason.

"Mom, would you and Dad mind taking

Brice into my office? I'd like to talk to Morgan alone for a minute."

When the conference-room door closed behind his parents, he turned to her. "That was pretty brutal. How are you holding up?"

"I'm fine."

Liar, he thought. But he didn't call her on it. He'd lied as well. By omission, when it came to Gil Rogers, but still.

"Look, Morgan, about the private investigator," he began.

She shook her head to stop his words. "Don't, Bryan. There's really no need for you to explain. I didn't know you'd hired one, but I knew that you didn't trust me. You made that pretty plain."

"In the beginning, yes. But that was before—"

Before he'd gotten to know her and realized what a strong, brave and determined woman she was.

Before he'd kissed her and his ordered world had begun spinning into chaos.

Before he'd fallen in love with her.

The last revelation was too new and staggering to ponder let alone share. Love? Good God! He hadn't seen it coming. Of course, he hadn't predicted any of the recent events that had occurred in his life.

Morgan was watching him, waiting for him to continue.

"I let past circumstances color my judgment. I meant it when I told the reporters you're nothing like my ex-wife. I should have seen that right away. I should have believed you."

"I understand, really." But her arms remained wrapped around her waist, her body language stating quite plainly that something was troubling her…something had hurt her.

"Still, I'm sorry. I made things more difficult for you in the beginning than they needed to be, especially given everything you were already going through. I know what happened to your parents."

"The detective?"

He nodded guiltily. "I can't even begin to imagine how horrible that must have been for you. And then, in my stubbornness, I cheated you and my parents out of months of time together."

That wasn't what he was most sorry for, though. Most of all, he was sorry about Dillon. Not only because his brother had lied to Morgan, charmed and seduced her in Aruba, and then walked away without a backward glance only to die in a tragic accident and leave her child fatherless. No. Bryan was sorry that Dillon had been the Caliborn brother to meet her first.

"It's okay. In the end, things have worked out the way they were meant to." Something in her words struck him as ominous, though he couldn't put a finger on what before she motioned toward the door and asked, "Do you think that's the end of it?"

"God, I hope so." Running a hand over the back of his neck, Bryan added, "I don't want to be dodging reporters' questions and pho-tographers' flashbulbs every time I leave the office or arrive home. That's why I tried to spell out the facts as clearly as possible so they won't look for more."

She offered what passed for a smile. "Well then, I'd say mission accomplished."

Immediately following the news conference, Morgan moved out of the penthouse as planned. Bryan moved back in. Her personal effects were gone, but reminders of her were everywhere. In the red accent pillows and throw, the scented candles and the dining-room-table runner she'd left behind. Even in the rearranged living-room furniture. She'd turned his place into a real home during the short time she'd lived there. But it didn't feel like a real home now that she and Brice were no longer in it. When he came home from work late the first evening she was gone, the penthouse just felt big and empty, and, yes, he could finally admit it, lonely.

He was lonely.

In the weeks that followed, it became clear that his relationship with Morgan had changed along with their addresses. Did she regret the stolen kisses they'd shared? She'd told him they should forget they'd ever happened and apparently she had. Bryan, however, hadn't been successful. He lay awake each night, torturing himself with memories of what had been as well as what he wished had transpired…what he still wished would happen. But none of it seemed possible when Morgan smiled at him so politely and kept him at a distance during visits that she made sure were conducted under the watchful eye of his parents.

It was killing him. She seemed not to notice.

CHAPTER ELEVEN

IN THE middle of November, Morgan found a house. She'd fallen in love with it at first sight. It was a two-story Tudor in a quiet, tree-lined neighborhood of older homes just a few miles from Bryan's parents' place. Compared to that house, it was small, but with four bedrooms and three and half baths spread over two stories, it more than accommodated her and Brice's needs.

It had a big yard with a couple of mature oaks whose fat limbs were perfect for supporting a tree house or a tire swing, and while the landscaping was nice, Morgan was sure Julia could give her plenty of ideas on how to improve it. The owners had already relocated to another state, which meant she could move in as soon as the paperwork was completed. If all went as planned, she and Brice could be in their own home by Thanksgiving or at the very least Christmas. The idea appealed to her. Even though she enjoyed staying in the guesthouse and the Caliborns respected her privacy, she wanted her own home, a place on which she was free to put her own stamp.

Today, Bryan was coming by to see the house. She'd asked him to, wanting his opinion since she would be plunking down a chunk of Brice's inheritance to pay for it. She waited for him in her car in the driveway. The vehicle was new, purchased a couple days after the old one had left her and the baby stranded in the rain. It was nothing flashy, but it boasted all of the latest safety features and had fared the best in a national publication's crash tests.

Leaves swirled on the street when Bryan pulled his Lexus to the curb. Morgan got out of her car and joined him on the brick-paved walk that led to the front door. He was dressed in a dark suit since he'd come straight from his office. His attire was professional, his smile personal. Upon seeing it, her pulse took off like a warning flare.

They hadn't been alone together since the press conference. Morgan had made sure of that. They wouldn't be alone for long now. Her real estate agent was running late, but the woman would be there any time to let them inside and answer his questions during the walk-through. Even so, Morgan wondered if it had been a mistake to leave Brice in the care of Bryan's parents. At least with the baby in her arms she wouldn't be so tempted to open hers to Bryan when he reached her.

"Hello, Morgan."

"Hi." The cool temperatures turned their greetings into white mist. They eyed one another awkwardly before she asked, "So, what do you think of the neighborhood?"

Stuffing his hands into his trouser pockets, he glanced around. "It's very solid. The values here are in no danger of dropping. And there's nothing wrong with the home's curb appeal."

"The mature trees help," she said, pointing to a nearby oak. Its leaves had turned yellow and most of them had fallen, exposing a squirrel's nest high in the thick branches.

"Brice is going to have a field day around here when he gets older."

"Tell me about it. He's already impatient to be mobile. Just this morning he pushed up onto his knees after rolling onto his belly. Any day now, he's going to be crawling and everything at his eye level will be fair game."

He glanced toward her car. "You didn't bring him?"

She shook her head. "He's with your mother."

The real estate agent arrived then. After apologizing for her lateness she unlocked the front door and waved them inside. "If it's okay with you, I'll just stay out here and make a few phone calls while you show Mr. Caliborn around."

Morgan swallowed. She had little choice but to agree. The door closed behind them with a thud that seemed to echo in the empty house.

"The parquet floors are original and for the most part in excellent shape."

"So I see."

She pointed to a room through an arched doorway to the side. "Why don't we start the tour in the dining room?"

Bryan had more on his mind than the house, but he followed her through the rooms, listening patiently and with no small amount of interest to her plans for decorating. It was clear Morgan loved the house. He liked it, too. Even though it was bare of furnishings and its walls were in need of a new coat of paint, it exuded charm and character. No doubt once she took possession of it, in short order and with little effort, she would turn it into a home.

Even now as they walked from space to space he could picture her there. In the living room sitting beside the fireplace and admonishing Brice to keep away from the flames. In the kitchen baking cookies or drinking hot cocoa at a table tucked into the nook. In the library curled up with Brice on an overstuffed couch turning the pages of a picture book.

And in the master bedroom at the top of the stairs, he pictured her in a big bed, wearing white satin and smiling as she held out her hand in invitation.

"What's wrong?"

Her question yanked Bryan from the day-dream. "Sorry?"

"You're frowning. Don't you like the house?"

"That's not it. The house is perfect. I can see you here," he told her truthfully.

The problem plaguing Bryan was he could see himself there, too. With Morgan. With Brice. And with the other children he wanted to create with her to fill up the spare bedrooms. He hadn't thought it possible to want a wife and children again after what had happened. He hadn't wanted to risk his heart as either a husband or a father. He knew the reason behind his changed mind. She was standing in front of him. She was also moving on. She didn't need him.

"Then you think I should buy it?" Morgan's excitement was palpable.

"Yes. It's a good investment, although I

wouldn't offer the full asking price given the current market."

"I was thinking the same thing," she replied. "Especially since the owners have already left and are motivated to sell."

He couldn't have asked for a better segue. Bryan cleared his throat. "Speaking of leaving, I'll be flying to London next week."

"The company's expansion project?" she guessed. She'd heard him and his father talk about it enough.

He nodded. "We've hit another snag. At this point the new facility won't be operational until next summer, which puts us six months behind schedule and close to three million dollars over budget. I'm hoping that by being there I can help move things along."

"How long will you be gone?"

"A month is the best-case scenario. Three or more if we need to appeal a judge's ruling."

Her expression dimmed. "You'll miss the holidays."

He shook his head, offered a crooked smile. "They have these things called airplanes, you know. But I will miss—"

Bryan couldn't stand it any longer. He had to touch her, even if just to stroke the side of her face, which he did. His hand lingered, turned so his palm could cradle her cheek. He didn't want the contact to end or the connection he felt with her staring up at him to be lost.

"What will you miss?" she asked softly.

"Seeing Brice on a regular basis. Babies change so fast." He swallowed. "And you, Morgan. I'll miss you."

His mouth found hers. The kiss was light, soft, giving her a chance to pull away if that's what she wanted. When she didn't, he infused it with all of the feelings he couldn't yet give voice to. Dillon had been good with words and a master when it came to persuasion. His brother also had been spontaneous, never thinking beyond the moment. Bryan couldn't be like that. He always looked before leaping. But he could be persuasive in his own way.

By the time the kiss ended, a plan was forming. He needed time to put it in place, to perfect his strategy. Twenty-four hours would do it.

"I have to go, Morgan, but can I stop by the guesthouse tomorrow evening?"

"Okay," she said slowly.

"Ask my mother to sit for Brice again. There's something we need to discuss."

Morgan blew out a breath and paced the length of the living room, hoping to wear off the worst of her nerves. Brice was already at the main house with the Caliborns, and Bryan was due to arrive at the guesthouse soon. She'd changed her clothes three times before deciding on a chocolate-brown sweater and tweed pants. She blamed her indecisiveness on the way he'd looked at her after that kiss.

Bryan could be a hard man to read, but as they'd stood in the empty master suite with the late-afternoon sun filtering through the window, she'd sworn a much deeper emotion had stirred in his dark gaze than the sort that went with either sexual attraction or family obligation. It had thrilled her to see it, especially coming as it had after his admission that he would miss her and Brice during his stay in London. But a moment later he'd been his usual contained self when he'd asked to stop by the guesthouse tonight.

She was adding a little more lip gloss when she heard the knock. She glanced at her watch. Bryan was early. Morgan wasn't sure what his eagerness said about the topic he wanted to "discuss."

"Hello, Morgan."

"Hi." She managed the greeting in a casual voice and stepped back to allow him inside. "Can I take your coat?"

He handed it to her along with the bottle of wine he'd brought. Morgan was still nursing Brice, but she decided to indulge in half a glass when she poured him some of the merlot. She'd expressed some breast milk earlier for Julia to give the baby and she'd begun supplementing his feedings with some formula and cereal so he slept through the night.

When she returned with their glasses, he was standing in front of the sofa. He took his glass of wine, but instead of sipping from it, he set it aside and then squared his shoulders as if preparing for battle. His tone was firm, his words more of an order rather than a request, when he said, "I want you and Brice to come to London with me."

"Wh-what?" Morgan's wine nearly sloshed over the rim at that. He took it from her hand and set it next to his on the side table.

"I know I won't be gone long, a matter of months at most, but I want you with me."

"You do?"

"Actually, I don't just want you with me in London, I want you to marry me, Morgan."

Her heart bucked out an extra beat as she waited for a declaration of love or at the very least a mention of his true feelings, but what Bryan said next was, "It makes sense for a number of reasons."

"Marriage makes sense?" she asked, because she wasn't sure she'd heard him right.

"Absolutely." He nodded, clasped his hands behind his back and began pacing in front of the sofa where she'd taken a seat since her legs threatened to give out. As if addressing Windy City's management team, Bryan began ticking off those reasons in a voice that conveyed plenty of conviction, but lacked the kind of passion a woman hopes to hear from a man asking her to spend the rest of her life with him.

"Brice is a Caliborn. He is an heir to one of the largest businesses in the country. It's not expected, but of course it's hoped, that when he comes of age he will take his place within the company that his great-great-grandfather started in post-fire Chicago."

"I'd never stand in the way of that."

"I love Brice. I know it took me a long time to show it, but it's true."

"You had your reasons," she said softly.

"I'd do anything for him." *Just as he would have done anything for Dillon?* "I want to look after him, Morgan." *Just as he'd always tried to look after Dillon?* "And I want to look after you." *Because Dillon was no longer there to do it?*

Responsibility, obligation, duty. Morgan needed better reasons than those to wed. "But marriage is—"

"The perfect solution."

His use of the word *solution* implied Bryan was addressing a problem. Her heart began to ache. The pain grew worse when he said, "You and I are compatible. I enjoy spending time with you." His gaze dipped to her lips. Longing, was that what she saw? Apparently not, she decided when he said, "We share similar tastes in takeout food and home furnishings."

Her eyes narrowed. "Chinese food and room decor are a good basis for a lifelong commitment?"

"That's not what I meant." He frowned, as if sensing his argument wasn't winning her over.

"It's just that a lot of couples I know got married because they were attracted to one another."

"And that's bad?"

"It's not enough. You have to have things in common to succeed long-term."

She agreed with him to an extent, but he still wasn't talking about love. Love was the only reason Morgan would marry.

"I will be faithful to you," he was saying. "Of course, I'll expect the same from you in return. And, as my wife, I will support you in whatever you want to do." He gestured with his arms. "For example, if you want to continue teaching music weekday afternoons at the south-side community center, you may do so."

"Gee, thanks for the permission."

He coughed. "What I mean is you wouldn't be limited to only that. I have the resources that would allow you to create your own center somewhere if you'd like, or do whatever else you feel necessary to bring music into the lives of young people." He ruined that fine speech by adding, "Philanthropy is a Caliborn trait."

"Apparently so is high-handedness." Morgan rose from the sofa. She'd heard enough. More than enough. Her heart couldn't take any more. Crossing her arms over her chest, she shouted, "Where do you get off telling me what I can do and expecting me to settle for compatibility in a marriage? When I marry—if I ever marry—it will be for love."

"But—"

She steamrollered over him. "As for Brice, you have no need to be concerned that I'll somehow deprive him of his heritage. As a matter of fact, I was already considering starting the necessary paperwork to legally change his last name from Stevens. As you said, he's a Caliborn. His name will reflect that soon enough."

"I didn't mean—"

"You didn't mean what? To insult me? To make me feel belittled and bullied? Well, you have. I thought—" She shook her head and shoved hurt behind anger. "It really doesn't matter what I thought now. I was wrong."

"It does matter."

She pointed a finger in the direction of the door. "Go, Bryan. Now. Because while you seem to think we have so much in common, at the moment I can't think of anything."

"Morgan—"

When he made no move to leave, she marched to the door, flung it wide for him.

"Just go. Maybe it's for the best you'll be leaving for London soon. I don't want to see you for a while. When you return, I'll be in my new home and things will be less awkward for all of us."

He stood at the threshold, looking dismayed. "You're angry with me."

The understatement grated. "And hugely disappointed." Hurt came into play, too. "But don't worry that how I feel right now is going to prevent me from allowing either you or your parents to see Brice. I came to Chicago because I wanted my child to have a relationship with his father's family. That hasn't changed. I may be a lot of things, but I can assure you that spiteful isn't one of them."

"I never thought that."

"Good." She nodded.

Frowning, he said, "I handled this wrong."

He was still *handling this wrong* as far as Morgan was concerned.

"Proposing marriage shouldn't make sense, Bryan. I know you've been hurt. I know what happened to you must have made it very hard for you to trust again. But marriage should be about love. You should want to marry the person you can't imagine living without. Not merely the person you feel an obligation to on behalf of your family."

She closed the door before he could respond. She didn't need to hear any more of his cold rationalizations.

He'd botched it. Screwed it up royally. He sat on one of the lounge chairs beside the pool and reran their conversation. He'd laid out his argument just as hc'd planned. It had sounded reasonable when he'd rehearsed it in front of the bathroom mirror earlier that day.

His head dropped forward and he scrubbed a hand over his face. *Reasonable.* God, he was an idiot. He walked to the main house, pausing outside the patio doors. Inside he could see his parents doting on Brice, who was lying on a blanket on the study floor.

They were happy again. Nothing could replace Dillon, of course. But the sharpest edges of their grief had been filed down thanks to the baby. Thanks to Morgan. She'd done the same for his grief, both over his brother and the boy he'd thought was his son.

She'd given them all a chance to get to know Brice when she could have filed a paternity suit and claimed compensation. In return she'd been doubted, dismissed, investigated and libeled.

If I ever marry—it will be for love.

The one thing Bryan had kept from her, even while seeking her hand. How cold it must have sounded, he thought as he climbed into his car and revved the engine to life. Hell, it must have sounded as if he were proposing a business merger rather than marriage.

CHAPTER TWELVE

FOR the next several days, Morgan was determined not to think about Bryan and his heartbreaking suggestion that they marry because it "made sense." She was hurt and angry with him. She also was disappointed with herself, because after he'd left she'd wondered if she should have said yes. She loved him. She wanted to be his wife.

To keep her mind off his proposal and her foolish heart, she immersed herself in the upcoming move. The owners had accepted the offer she'd made, leaving only the paperwork and packing to complete. Morgan was looking forward to retrieving the rest of her belongings from storage and having the new piano she'd purchased delivered. At the penthouse, she'd had Bryan's baby grand to play. Other than at the community center, she hadn't played in weeks.

Before she could move in, however, some work had to be done, thankfully all of it cosmetic and not likely to take very long. She'd hired a painter and was in the process of picking out wall colors, had measured the windows for custom shades and draperies and had made inquires to have the hardwood floor in the living room refinished. If all went according to plan, she and Brice would be out of the guesthouse the first week in December.

Bryan would already be in London. Morgan sat down at the counter with a bundle of paint chips and tried not to think about the fact that he was leaving that day. She wasn't very successful. She could only hope that by the time he flew in for Christmas, she'd have her emotions under control.

When she glanced up and saw him outside the door that led to the patio, she almost thought she was imagining things. But he knocked then and the sound had her scrambling off the stool.

"What are you doing here?" She glanced at her watch. "Your flight leaves for London in less than three hours. Shouldn't you be on your way to the airport?"

"I should be," he agreed. "But I couldn't leave without seeing you."

Morgan's heart, bruised but apparently still foolish, knocked against her ribs. Tell him to go, her head demanded. Her feet didn't obey. Stepping back, she invited him inside. He was, after all, her son's uncle. If he could be pragmatic about their relationship, then so could she.

"So, besides seeing me, what brings you here?" She gave herself high marks for her casual tone and blasé attitude. They provided a nice cover for her clammy palms and rioting nerves.

"You and I have some unfinished business that needs settling." He shook his head then and grimaced. "Not business. Forget I used that word. What's between us is personal."

"I think we already *discussed* everything we needed to discuss when you were here the other night."

Having picked up on her emphasis on the other offending word he'd used, he told her, "No discussion this time, Morgan. I'm here to apologize."

"Okay." She crossed her arms, a reminder to herself to hold firm. "I'm listening."

He blew out a breath, looking uncharacteristically nervous. "Oh, hell, I'm no good at this."

Genuinely curious, she asked, "At what?"

"Talking." He gestured with one hand. "Oh, sure, with cue cards or memorized responses, I can come off well enough. But when I have to speak extemporaneously—" he cleared his throat "—or from the heart, I don't do so well."

Her eyebrows inched up. "I promise not to grade you."

"Right. The other night when I came here, I knew what I wanted, but my approach was all wrong. I left you with the impression that my ultimate goal was to provide for you and Brice."

"It's not?"

"No. Well, yes. Of course I want to provide for you. But that's not why—" He swore again and then reached for the fan of paint chips. "I want to marry you, Morgan, because I don't want to come home to a beige penthouse any longer. My life is beige. I want color in it. And, before you say it, I'm not talking about home decor here."

When she opened her mouth to speak, he waved a hand to stop her.

"That sounds corny. Forget it. What I meant to say is I'm lonely." He winced. "God, that makes me sound desperate and as if just anyone would do. But that's not true. I am lonely, but I don't want to be alone anymore and you're the reason."

Before she could respond, he blew out a sigh. "I'm making an ass of myself when I'm trying to sweep you off your feet. I need you. I don't want to lose you, because I love you, Morgan. I love you and Brice. And I want us to be a real family."

She put a hand over her mouth, holding in a sob and unintentionally covering up her smile. He loved her. The passion in his tone and his perfectly imperfect proposal made that clear.

"Aren't you going to say anything?" he asked.

She crossed to where he stood. For the first time since she'd known him Bryan didn't look authoritative, imposing or powerful. His expression was unguarded and sincere enough to steal her breath. Maybe that was why it took her so long to speak.

"Well?" he prodded, looking like a newly convicted man awaiting his sentence.

Morgan decided to put him out of his misery. "I have just one thing to say." Going up on tiptoe, she wound her arms around his neck. A moment before her lips touched his, she murmured, "It looks like we're going to have to call another press conference."

MILLS & BOON PUBLISH EIGHT LARGE PRINT TITLES A MONTH. THESE ARE THE EIGHT TITLES FOR DECEMBER 2009.

THE SICILIAN'S BABY BARGAIN
Penny Jordan

MISTRESS: PREGNANT BY THE SPANISH BILLIONAIRE
Kim Lawrence

BOUND BY THE MARCOLINI DIAMONDS
Melanie Milburne

BLACKMAILED INTO THE GREEK TYCOON'S BED
Carol Marinelli

CATTLE BARON: NANNY NEEDED
Margaret Way

GREEK BOSS, DREAM PROPOSAL
Barbara McMahon

BOARDROOM BABY SURPRISE
Jackie Braun

BACHELOR DAD ON HER DOORSTEP
Michelle Douglas